"Please, Tander, just go. Leave me alone," Amnity pleaded.

"No. I won't push you, but there's no way I'm walking out of your life."

"I don't want what you do. Please, go now."

"I'm a patient man. I'll wait as long as I have to."

Amnity sighed. "You are an infuriating man, and used to having things your own way with women. Well, not this time. It takes two to . . . to . . ."

"Tango?" he suggested.

She pointed to the door. "Go!"

He moved to stand so close to her, he could almost hear her heart pounding wildly. "I'll go, but the memory of what we just shared—of what we will share again—will stay with you, Amnity. You're not getting rid of me easily. Nothing like this has ever happened to me before, lady. I'll be back. . . ."

WHAT ARE *LOVESWEPT* ROMANCES?

They are stories of true romance and touching emotion. We believe those two very important ingredients are constants in our highly sensual and very believable stories in the *LOVESWEPT* line. Our goal is to give you, the reader, stories of consistently high quality that may sometimes make you laugh, sometimes make you cry, but are always fresh and creative and contain many delightful surprises within their pages.

Most romance fans read an enormous number of books. Those they truly love, they keep. Others may be traded with friends and soon forgotten. We hope that each *LOVESWEPT* romance will be a treasure—a "keeper." We will always try to publish

LOVE STORIES YOU'LL NEVER FORGET
BY AUTHORS YOU'LL ALWAYS REMEMBER

The Editors

LOVESWEPT® • 398

Joan Elliott Pickart
Whispered Wishes

BANTAM BOOKS
NEW YORK · TORONTO · LONDON · SYDNEY · AUCKLAND

WHISPERED WISHES

A Bantam Book / May 1990

LOVESWEPT® and the wave device are registered
trademarks of Bantam Books, a division of
Bantam Doubleday Dell Publishing Group, Inc.
Registered in U.S. Patent
and Trademark Office and elsewhere.

If you would be interested in receiving protective vinyl
covers for your Loveswept books, please write to this address
for information:

Loveswept
Bantam Books
P.O. Box 985
Hicksville, NY 11802

ISBN 0-553-44029-2

Published simultaneously in the United States and Canada

Bantam Books are published by Bantam Books, a division
of Bantam Doubleday Dell Publishing Group, Inc. Its trademark, consisting of the words "Bantam Books" and the
portrayal of a rooster, is Registered in U.S. Patent and
Trademark Office and in other countries. Marca Registrada.
Bantam Books, 666 Fifth Avenue, New York, New York 10103.

PRINTED IN THE UNITED STATES OF AMERICA

OPM   0 9 8 7 6 5 4 3 2 1

For Sylvia, Ikie, and Virginia

One

"Amnity, dear," the elderly woman said, "please tell my friend Sally the enchanting story that goes with that favorite quilt of yours, the one hanging there on the wall. Amnity won't sell it, Sally, so just save your breath. I've asked and asked."

Amnity Ames smiled at the two women. "You know that story as well as I do, Mrs. Ferguson."

"Oh, I realize that," Melissa Ferguson said, "but you tell it so much better than I can. Such a treasure that quilt is, Sally. Amnity found it at an estate auction down South. It's a signal quilt."

"A what?" Sally asked.

"Go on, Amnity," Melissa said. "Tell Sally the story about the quilt."

Amnity laughed at the same time that the antique copper bell over the door of her shop, the Crazy Quilt, rang, announcing someone's arrival. A gust of damp, chill wind that was typical for mid-February on the Virginia coast accompanied the new customer.

Amnity turned to greet the visitor and felt her smile fade into oblivion. A man had entered the Crazy Quilt, which in itself was a rare occurrence. The few men who came into the shop were usually with their wives, and had a tendency to appear totally bored and grimly put-upon.

But this man, Amnity realized, was alone. And he was, without a doubt, the most handsome man she'd ever seen.

Probably in his early thirties, he was tall, at least six feet, with broad shoulders, a deep tan, and tousled sun-streaked hair. The line of his jaw and cheek seemed chiseled from stone, yet his lips looked soft, sensuous.

Across the width of the store, though, the color of his eyes was a mystery. Were they blue? she wondered. Brown? Or maybe they were . . .

Oh, for heaven's sake! she admonished herself. She was acting like an adolescent. It wasn't like her to stare at a handsome man, or at any man, for that matter. It was time she exhibited at least a modicum of professional decorum.

"Hello," she said, producing her smile again. "May I help you?"

"Yes, dear," Melissa Ferguson said. "Assist the gentleman, then please tell Sally the story of the signal quilt."

"I'm in no rush," the man said. "Go ahead with your story. I'll wait."

"Thank you, young man," Melissa said, beaming. "You'll enjoy this story, too. I'm sure. It's about that signal quilt hanging there on the wall. Amnity?"

She liked the man's voice, Amnity was thinking. It was deep and rich, and she could imagine that voice calling a woman's name . . .

"Amnity?"

"Oh, yes, of course, the story," Amnity said, pulling her gaze from the compelling stranger. "That quilt was, indeed, a signal quilt back in the days of the Underground Railroad that led freedom-seeking slaves to safety in the North. The colors and design of the quilt broadcast the message that a certain station was safe. The quilt was draped over a bench or a tree limb, anywhere that it could be easily seen. Those involved in helping the slaves could read the message of the quilt as clearly as they might a printed sign. It's wonderful when you realize that a quilt, painstakingly made by hand, stitch by stitch, was the means by which hundreds of people gained their freedom."

"Isn't that marvelous?" Sally said. "That tale is fascinating, and very touching."

"I told you so," said Melissa, obviously pleased with herself. "That story thrills me every time I hear it. Oh, dear, look at the hour. I'd best get that thread I need, so we can be on our way to meet Elaine for lunch. I know just where my thread is, Amnity, so you don't have to fuss with us. We're going over against that far wall, Sally. Isn't this just the cutest shop?"

Amnity watched as the two women crossed the store, then glanced around. Yes, she thought, it was a cute shop, and she was very proud of it. The Crazy Quilt was her dream come true, a marvelous store, born of many hours of hard work. She sold all sorts of supplies for making various crafts, with special emphasis on quilts. Displayed on the walls and shelves were different items she had made herself, and she also conducted classes in quilting.

"Nice story," the man said.

His deep voice jerked her from her momentary daydreaming. She looked at him, and was once again amazed by his incredible good looks and strong build. Her heart did a funny little tap dance, which she decided to ignore.

"Now then," she said, "how may I help you?"

He started toward her, and she realized he was leaning on an ornately carved wooden cane and walking with a pronounced limp.

What had happened to him? she wondered. He was obviously in superb condition, except for the limp. Had he been in an accident? When? Was it a temporary injury?

Stop it! she told herself. It wasn't like her to delve, even mentally, into other people's business, and she certainly didn't speculate about total strangers.

"I'm looking for—" he started, then stopped as Melissa and Sally bustled back to the counter. "I'll browse for a minute."

"All right," Amnity said, watching him move slowly toward the interior of the shop. "I'll be able to help you in just a moment."

"I found my thread, Amnity," Melissa said. "I'm going to bring Sally back on another day, when we can stay longer. She's deciding if she wants to sign up for the quilting class I'm enrolled in. You still have room for more students, don't you?"

"Yes, there's space for a few more," Amnity said. "Don't wait too long, though, to decide.

Those classes have been full every time I've given them."

"Did you hear that, Sally?" Melissa said. "Well, for now, I'll pay for my thread, and we'll be on our way. Elaine fusses so if a person is even five minutes late."

Melissa and Sally were soon hurrying out the door, sending the old copper bell to tinkling. As Amnity glanced around to determine where the man had gone, she was acutely aware of the silence in the shop.

It was too quiet, she thought.

She shook her head at her own foolishness, and smoothed the skirt of her mint-green lightweight wool dress over her hips. A dress that suddenly felt too warm.

She was acting ridiculously, she chided herself. She'd been in the company of handsome men before, and this particular man was simply a customer of the Crazy Quilt. Oh, who was she kidding? He was the best-looking customer ever to open the door and bring his scrumptious self into her store.

Telling herself to concentrate on business, she spotted the man over by the yarn and started toward him.

He replaced a skein of orange yarn and picked up a yellow one, only to set it back on the shelf a moment later. He met her gaze as she neared him.

Amnity stopped in front of him, seeing at last that his eyes were brown, with the most amazing flecks of amber in them. The slightly questioning look in those eyes recalled her to business.

"May I help you find something?" she asked.

He nodded. "I hope so."

"Are you looking for a particular item?" He even smelled good, she thought. He was wearing a musky after-shave that was neither too sweet nor too heavy, but seemed perfect for him. "Let me introduce myself. I'm Amnity Ames, the owner of the Crazy Quilt." She laughed. "I know where everything is, because I've spent hours putting it all in place." She paused, cocking her head to one side. "Sir?"

"What? Oh, sorry, I was thinking." He flashed her a dazzling smile. "My being in this kind of store is my doctor's idea, and I really don't know what I'm actually looking for."

"Your doctor told you to come to a crafts shop?"

"Yes. You see, I'm recuperating from knee surgery that was required after an automobile accident. The truth is, Miss Ames . . . It is Miss, isn't it?" he asked, raising his eyebrows.

"Yes, it is." She paused. "Mr. . . . ?" What

on earth was she doing? She didn't need to know his name.

"Ellis. Tander Ellis."

"Well, Mr.—Mr. Ellis," she said, deciding to look at a spot just above his right shoulder, "perhaps if you could tell me what your doctor said, I would be better able to help you. As you can see, the Crazy Quilt carries a wide variety of crafts. We have everything from kits for the beginner to extremely complex endeavors. There are also supplies for those who prefer to create their own crafts. For example—"

"Amnity?"

"I . . . yes?" Her name spoken in that deep, rich voice sounded different from how it had ever sounded before, and strangely sensual. Something about the way Tander Ellis said her name caused a fluttering along her spine, and a swirling sensation in her stomach. A hot swirling sensation. Dear Lord, what was this man doing to her? "Mr. Ellis, just what exactly did your doctor suggest for you to do?"

"Tander. You call me Tander, and I'll call you Amnity. That's because you have a lovely, unusual name, and I like saying it."

And she liked hearing it, she thought. Oh, Amnity, please. Stop it this very instant.

"All right, Amnity?"

"Yes, that's fine," she said, still not meeting his gaze.

"Do I make you nervous for some reason?"

She looked at him then, and lifted her chin slightly.

"No, of course not," she said, a bit of an edge to her voice. "There's certainly no reason why you would make me nervous, Mr. . . . Tander. Now, suppose you explain just how I can help you."

"It's very simple, really," he said. "I've been out of commission for a month already with this knee, and have weeks to go before I'm up to par. I'm going nuts sitting around. There are just so many hours in any given day that a guy can read, watch television, do crossword puzzles. I'm in physical therapy now, but I still spend a lot of time on my backside doing nothing. My doctor said that needlepoint is very relaxing, while offering a challenge at the same time. I think this is a bit flaky, but I'm admittedly becoming a desperate man."

"Your doctor is absolutely right, and there are published reports on the subject. So, you need a needlepoint kit. I suggest you start with something easy so that you don't become frustrated, thereby defeating the purpose of why you're doing it. My policy at the Crazy Quilt, though, is to offer assistance to anyone who needs it after they've purchased their materials here. Do feel free to come by any time . . . during store hours."

"That's comforting," Tander said, chuckling. "I have a feeling I'm going to need all the help I can get with this project."

"Let's go to the needlepoint section, shall we?" Amnity spun around and started away. Would he come back for help with the needlepoint? she wondered. Would she ever see Tander Ellis again? Why was she asking herself these questions? Moreover, why was the idea of seeing Tander again so tantalizing? "Needlepoint," she said, halting and sweeping one arm in the air.

Tander limped up to her and stopped. "Lord," he said, "there're dozens of them. For someone who doesn't know diddly about this stuff, it's rather overwhelming."

"Not really, Tander. I have them in order of difficulty. This first group is for beginners. The colored picture on the package shows you what the finished project will look like, and you have a wide variety to choose from. Do you see anything that strikes your fancy?"

"Well," he said, peering at the many kits, "I guess I'll take the one with the rainbow."

"Wishes on rainbows," she said softly. She slid the package off the hook and stared at the vibrant rainbow on the front. "This is one of my favorite kits."

"Do you?" Tander asked, his voice low as he gazed at her intently.

She shifted her eyes to meet his. "Do I what?"

"Do you make wishes on rainbows?"

"I . . ."

There was not, Amnity realized, enough air in her lungs to complete an entire sentence. Her heartbeat had quickened to a wild tempo that echoed in her ears. The curling sensation of heat returned, pulsing low within her as she was held immobile by Tander Ellis's mesmerizing gaze. A flicker of excitement swept through her, but was quickly followed and chased away by fear.

"No," she whispered, then forced strength into her voice. "No, I don't make wishes on rainbows, Mr. Ellis. Not anymore. Here's your needlepoint kit," she added, nearly shoving it at him. "All the supplies you'll need, plus the instructions, are in there. Good luck. I hope you enjoy your new project."

He smiled at her as he took the kit. "Well, we'll see how this goes. Don't be surprised if I show up a lot, screaming for help. The Crazy Quilt will probably become my second home. You'll get tired of seeing me around here."

No, she wouldn't, Amnity thought. She

wouldn't tire of seeing Tander Ellis, hearing his voice, standing close enough to him to feel faintly the heat of his body. Excitement surged through her again at the idea of him coming time after time to the Crazy Quilt. He was having a powerful sensual affect on her on a level of man-to-woman, and that realization, while thrilling, was also terribly upsetting.

She did not want to be feeling this strange and shockingly strong attraction to Tander. For almost all of the time she'd been on her own, she'd kept her contacts with men on a friendly basis. She wasn't interested in a serious involvement with a man. She had no intention of ever again placing her emotional well-being in the hands of another.

Therefore, she vowed, whatever this unexpected and unwelcome schoolgirlish reaction to Tander Ellis was, it was over as of this very second.

"Well now," she said brightly, "you're all set." She turned and started back toward the front counter. "I'm sure you'll do just fine with your rainbow kit. Just remember to be patient and not rush it until you get the hang of making the stitches. You'll find that—"

"Amnity."

His voice was so low, yet held such a quality of authority and command, Amnity stopped dead in her tracks. Sensual heat pulsed deep within her, flushing her cheeks.

"Amnity," he said again, "wait."

No! she thought, though she didn't move. She mustn't wait for someone like Tander Ellis. He was a man of control, she could sense it. Even with his injured leg, there was a vitality and intensity emanating from him, along with a potent sexuality.

He possessed the power to manipulate, to obtain what he wanted with ease, with bone-melting smiles and never-ending charm. Women fell prey to men like Tander, and she had no intention of being one of them.

"With this bum knee," he said, coming up behind her, "I can't walk as fast as you can. That's why I asked you to wait."

She blinked, then turned to face him. "Oh. Yes, of course, I'm sorry. I wasn't thinking."

He smiled. "Well, I'm the stubborn type, you see. I wasn't exactly thrilled about the idea of doing needlepoint, but now that I've decided to go for it, I'll give it my best shot. The way you were practically sprinting, I was afraid you'd divulge an inside tip or two that I'd miss because you were too far ahead of me." His smile faded. "Once I've made up my mind about something, Amnity, I become very determined."

A shiver coursed through her. "Do you always get your own way?"

"The majority of the time. Especially when it's extremely important to me." His voice seemed to drop an octave. "Understand?"

Amnity knew they were no longer talking about needlepoint. She could see the desire smoldering in the depths of Tander's eyes, could hear the veiled meaning behind his supposedly innocent words. Tander Ellis wanted her. On a purely male-and-female level, he was making that perfectly clear.

"No one," she said, meeting his gaze directly, "wins all of the time, Mr. Ellis. I'm sure you're intelligent enough to realize that. However, in the case of your learning needlepoint, I see no problem with your succeeding. You should complete a very lovely rainbow. Shall I ring that kit up for you, or would you like to browse a while longer?"

"I don't need anything else," he said. He paused for a second, then added, "Today."

Damn the man, Amnity thought, as she started toward the counter again. He had to have the last word, the last little zinger. She wanted Tander Ellis out of her shop that very minute.

Without looking directly at him, she rang up the cost of the kit on the cash register, accepted a bill from him, gave him his change, and slipped the kit into a perky calico-print paper bag.

"Thank you," she said, "and enjoy your project. Good day, Mr. Ellis."

She began to straighten a stack of flyers that advertised her upcoming quilting classes. Flyers that were in no need of straightening.

"I'll be back, Amnity," Tander said quietly, "very soon."

Her head snapped up, and she looked at him warily. "Oh?"

He smiled, a slow, lazy, all-male smile. "Yep, I'll be back. I intend to complete this rainbow, but that's not to say I won't need some help with it. You did guarantee that I'd be welcome here whenever I became . . . frustrated. See ya." He turned and walked slowly toward the door, leaning heavily on the cane.

What a despicable man, Amnity fumed. He always had one more thing to say, and it invariably had a sexual innuendo woven through it. Did he think she was a naive child who wasn't catching his double entendres? No, he was very aware that she understood everything he was saying. He was—

The bell over the door tinkled.

He was gone.

Amnity stared at the door for a long moment before she realized a knot had tightened painfully in her stomach. She felt strange, as though she were being pulled in two directions at once.

Part of her wanted to rush after Tander and tell him she wasn't ready for him to leave, to take the warmth from the room and the heat of desire from her body. She wanted a few more minutes to be so incredibly aware of her own femininity and of his virility. She wanted to look at him and imagine what it would be like to be held in those strong arms, kissed by his sensuous lips. To lose herself in the sensations he would create within her . . .

But the other part of her violently rejected that. Tander Ellis was gone, having done nothing more than spend a handful of minutes in her shop like any other customer. She was overreacting.

And that, Amnity told herself, was that.

She walked slowly through the store, fiddling with crafts supplies and fussing with displays that didn't need her attention. She glanced often at the door, wishing a customer would come in, someone she could talk to and break the almost eerie silence that had fallen over the Crazy Quilt.

It was just so quiet in there.

The bell over the door tinkled, and three women came in, chattering and laughing.

Sighing with relief, Amnity pushed her distressing thoughts to a dusty corner of her mind, planted her best smile on her face, and walked forward to greet her customers.

Tander sank into the plush leather sofa in the main lounge of his yacht and stared at the telephone. Running his hand over the back of his neck, he muttered several earthy expletives.

The telephone was jabbing at his conscience, telling him to make the call he should have placed when he arrived back at the yacht an hour before.

He'd make the call, he told himself, in a minute. Just as soon as he squared things away in his mind with regard to Amnity Ames. The fact that he'd been attempting to do that for over an hour was not improving his rapidly deteriorating mood.

Yes, Amnity Ames was a beautiful woman, but so were a lot of other women. More intriguing was the glimpse of vulnerability he'd seen beneath the outer demeanor of the self-assured businesswoman. The glimpse of a fragile bird.

The photograph he'd seen of her hadn't done her justice. Not by a long shot. Her shoulder-length black hair was cut in a simple but attractive style, and her eyes were an unusual shade of gray. With her slender figure, lovely face, and long, long legs, she was a very appealing woman. And her laughter was as clear and delightful as the tinkling of the copper bell over the door of her shop.

"Damn," he said, shaking his head.

He glowered at the telephone, then snatched up the receiver. He punched in a series of numbers, then drummed the fingers of one hand on the table as the ringing began on the other end of the line. Halfway through the third ring, a deep voice said, "Santini."

"Vince? Tander."

"Good. I've been waiting for your call. I didn't think it would take this long to establish contact with Amnity Ames."

Tander rolled his eyes. He was not about to tell Vince about the hour he'd spent chasing his own thoughts around in his mind.

"So?" Vince asked. "How did it go? Did you charm the socks off the lady? Is she putty in your hands, hotshot?"

"Can it, Santini," Tander snapped. "I got the layout of the shop, okay? I've met Amnity, bought a needlepoint kit, and paved the way to go back for help working on the stupid thing. Satisfied?"

"Hey, whoa, what's your problem? You're uptight about something, Tander."

Dammit, Tander thought, this was exactly

why he'd postponed making the call. He'd been afraid Vince would discern his mood, even over the phone. Of course, biting Santini's head off wasn't too bright.

"Tander?"

"I'm here. I'm sorry I was short with you, Vince. I'm a tad out of practice as far as this stuff goes, I guess. I retired years ago, you know, intending to live the life of the decadent rich. So, what happens? You quit the L.A. Police Department, start your own private agency, end up working with the feds, and snag me to do an assignment for you."

"Becoming a private investigator was the best decision of my life, buddy. Except for marrying Katha, of course. And you were eager to take this job when I called you. If your less-than-chipper mood indicates that you want out, say so now, before I have to retrace too many of your steps. Time is important on this, Tander."

"I realize that. Listen, I'm in for the duration, Vince, so don't worry about it. It's just taking a few mental adjustments on my part to get used to working again."

"That's understandable. Being out in the field must be a jolt after all this time, but you're perfect for this one." Vince paused. "The contact with Amnity Ames really went all right?"

"Yes. It went fine."

"Good. Remember, watch your back."

"Count on it, Vince."

"Call me when you have something to report."

"Yep. 'Bye."

In Los Angeles, in a large, nicely furnished office, Vincent Santini slowly hung up the phone. He didn't remove his hand, but stared at the receiver, a deep frown on his face.

No, forget it, he decided. He was worrying about Tander's strange mood for no reason. Tander was Tander. And Tander Ellis was always in control.

He was, Tander realized, out of control. When he'd worked for the government several years earlier, he'd always been calm, cool, and deadly. His personal feelings never entered the picture when he was on assignment. So why couldn't he forget Amnity Ames's softly appealing gray eyes, her timid smiles, or delightful laughter?

It didn't matter, he told himself. Amnity Ames was driving him nuts, causing him to lose it, and he'd had enough. Whatever crazy spell she'd cast over him, it no longer existed. He was taking charge of his mind and body again. He'd adjusted to working an assignment; he was ready to roll.

Tander surged to his feet and began to pace the large room, decorated with brass fixtures, mahogany tables, and expensive leather chairs and sofas.

And as he strode back and forth with long, forceful strides, there was no hint of a limp.

Two

A string of expletives disrupted the pleasant jazz that floated through the main lounge of Tander's yacht. He held the needlepoint canvas at arm's length, squinted at it, swore at it, then dropped it next to him on the sofa.

Just dandy, he thought, lunging to his feet. His plan had been to *pretend* that he was having difficulty making the small stitches described in the directions in the kit, then return to the Crazy Quilt to ask for Amnity's help.

He crossed the room with thudding strides, his bare feet sinking into the thick carpet. He poured himself a cup of coffee, then scowled into the steaming liquid.

After one solid hour laboring over that idiotic rainbow, he had six stitches completed; three at one angle, three going the other way. The instructions specifically stated that the stitches should all slant in the same direction. He was being reduced to a mass of tense, aching muscles because of a crummy, maddening needlepoint rainbow.

Wishes on rainbows, he thought suddenly. That was what Amnity had said in a soft, wistful voice as she'd gazed at the picture on the kit. He'd seen her vulnerability at that moment, before she'd slipped her cool, professional facade back into place.

There was more to Amnity Ames than met the eye, he mused. Not that what met the eye wasn't very appealing. But there was more to Amnity, hidden beneath the surface that she presented. An intriguing and beautiful woman, was Miss Amnity Elizabeth Ames.

And guilty as sin? Was she involved in her brother's illegal activities?

Tander set the china cup down and returned to the sofa. Leaning his head back on the soft upholstery, he stared at the ceiling.

Was Amnity Ames the partner of Andrew Ames, her thirty-two-year-old brother, four years older than she and with a rap sheet as long as Tander's arm? Was Amnity Ames, who no longer made wishes on rainbows, a criminal?

Tander didn't know, and it was his job to find out. The assignment also included snaring the elusive Mr. Andrew Ames, and obtaining possession of stolen diamonds that, according to an informant, Ames intended to smuggle into the United States.

In a dark alley in Greece, the informant had met with an American agent. The whispered message had included Amnity's name, and the words "Crazy Quilt." The informant didn't know Amnity's role in the smuggling operation. He'd only overheard her name and that of her store.

Tander shifted his gaze to the picture of the vibrant rainbow that lay next to him.

Tander knew he wanted Amnity to be simply the beautiful, intriguing woman he'd met the day before in her cozy shop. The woman with laughter that danced through the air, and who had eyes as soft as a kitten's fur. He did not want her to be her brother's accomplice.

Shape up, Ellis, he told himself. If Amnity was guilty, he'd haul her in right along with her brother. She was nothing more than a piece of the puzzle Vince was counting on him to solve. *Nothing more.*

Then why, Tander asked himself with a weary sigh, had he put on a sweater that was the exact shade of Amnity Ames's beautiful gray eyes?

• • •

As the copper bell over the door announced that someone was entering the Crazy Quilt, Amnity's head snapped up and her heart began to beat rapidly. Releasing a pent-up breath, she smiled at the woman who had come in and nodded when she said she wanted to browse.

Darn it, Amnity thought, she'd done it again. During that entire day, she'd tensed every time the copper bell had chimed.

She'd been watching for Tander Ellis.

She'd admitted that halfway through the day, and was thoroughly appalled at herself. Finally, though, it was five minutes to six. At six o'clock, she could lock up the store, go home to a relaxing bubble bath, and escape Tander's haunting image. If that mental picture of him followed her home, as it had done the previous night, she was going to scream in angry frustration.

Nothing like this had ever happened to her before, and it was disconcerting, to say the least. Why had Tander Ellis had such a sensual impact on her? You'd think she'd never talked to a man before.

Well, she reasoned, maybe there was something in that. She'd met him in the Crazy Quilt, a shop that was frequented almost entirely by women. She'd overreacted to Tander's masculinity simply because she was unaccustomed to a man of his good looks and virility being in her store.

It made sense, she told herself, and now she could handle Tander without difficulty the next time she saw him.

The copper bell tinkled, and she mentally patted herself on the back as she took her time looking toward the door, smiling a pleasant, welcoming smile.

Oh, dear Lord, she thought. Tander Ellis has just come into the Crazy Quilt. She could feel her heart pounding, the sudden warmth on her cheeks . . .

No, she told herself. She had this under control. If her body would just catch up with her rational mind, she'd be in great shape.

"Hello, Tander," she said, a bit too brightly.

"Amnity," he said, inclining his head.

He stood just inside the door, leaning on his cane, the calico-print bag tucked under his left arm. She started instinctively to walk toward him, when her attention was diverted by the three remaining customers in the store, all eager to make their purchases before she closed for the evening. She rang up their sales, wished the ladies a pleasant good night, then watched the last woman leave the shop.

"I didn't realize it was so late," Tander said, smiling. Not true, he thought. He'd carefully timed his arrival at the Crazy Quilt. "I was wandering through some of the other stores in this complex. The candle place, the glass shop." Also not true. He'd read a report on the fifteen businesses housed in the buildings that were arranged to suggest a small village. Lies. So many lies. "Well, I'm out of luck for today, I guess. I'll get going, so you can lock up." He turned toward the door.

"No, wait," Amnity said. Wait? she wondered. What was she saying? The Crazy Quilt was closed, all customers should be gone. Tander Ellis was a customer, nothing more. What did she want him to wait for? "Was there something specific you wanted?"

Oh, Amnity, Tander thought dryly. That was a very loaded question. His mind picked up the enticing ball and ran with it down a road that had his libido screaming for mercy.

"My rainbow is a mess," he said, producing his most dazzling smile. "All six stitches of it. You could torture me, and I'd never divulge how long it took me to make these six lousy stitches."

"Oh, dear," Amnity said, laughing softly. "Why don't I take a look at it? I don't mind staying a few extra minutes. Just let me lock up, so that no one else wanders in." Walking from behind the counter, she started across the room toward him.

Sensational, he thought, his gaze flickering over her. Her pale blue sweater did fantastic things for her shiny dark hair and her incredible eyes. The darker blue wool skirt flattered her shapely calves and ankles. Amnity Ames was very, very beautiful. And he'd like a fin for every time he'd thought that in the past day.

Amnity walked past Tander to the door, inhaling the scent of his after-shave as she went. Realizing her hands were trembling as she locked up, she wondered again why she had invited him to stay. It was foolish, risky. She had no business being alone with Tander, knowing the disturbing effect he had on her. Five minutes, she decided. She'd allow herself five minutes, maximum, to examine his rainbow, then she'd bid him good night and send him on his way.

"All finished," she said, turning to face him. "I'll take a look at your famous six stitches now."

He glanced at his cane, then the bag tucked under his arm. "Grab the bag, will you? I've run out of hands at the moment."

"Oh, well . . . yes, of course," she said.

She lifted one hand, then hesitated. What would it be like, she wondered, to run her hand over Tander's chest, to feel the hard muscles beneath her palm, the strength in his taut, powerful body? What would it be like to inch his sweater upward and— Amnity Ames, shame on you. Take the stupid bag.

She snatched the bag, and Tander blinked in surprise at her abrupt action.

Oh, good Lord, she thought, pulling the needlepoint canvas out, the bag was warm from being held so close to his body. It seemed to be actually singeing her fingers with its heat. Tander's heat. And she was going to be carted away to the funny farm for getting all in a dither over a paper sack.

"Well . . . yes. Um . . . these are certainly very interesting stitches you have here, Tander." She cringed inwardly at the squeaky sound of her voice. "All six of them."

"Yeah, I know," he said, with an overly dramatic sigh. "I have three going in one direction, and three in another. That rainbow is driving me nuts."

She peered more closely at the canvas. "If I didn't know better, I'd think you'd done one set of three with your left hand, and the other set with your right."

He nodded. "That's possible. I really don't remember. I'm ambidextrous, and I never think about which hand I'm using at the moment."

"That's it," she said, smiling as she met his gaze. "That's the solution to your problem. A left-handed person's stitches slant in the opposite direction from someone who is right-handed. If you switch back and forth, you're going to have a—"

"Mess," he said, matching her smile. "Okay, Coach, I get it. I'll pick one hand and stick with it. All I have to do is remember which hand it is."

"Precisely." She slid the canvas back into the bag, then extended it toward him.

"Tuck it under my arm, would you, please?"

Don't think about his chest, she told herself. Slide the bag into place, and do *not* think. "Certainly." She whipped the sack under his arm, then quickly stepped back. "There you go. You're all set."

"I appreciate your help." He paused. "Listen, it's dinnertime, and we both have to eat. Why don't we go somewhere for supper?"

"No, I don't think that's a . . ." She stopped. It *was* a good idea, because she would be with Tander in an environment other than her ultrafeminine shop. She'd be able to put him, as a man, in proper perspective if they were in a restaurant with other men. There was some risk involved, spending an evening with a tantalizing man like Tander, but it could put an end to her ridiculous reactions to him. "Actually, I'd enjoy that," she amended. "I'll get my coat."

"I'm in the mood for some seafood," he said. "Do you know a good place near here? Do you like seafood?"

"I love it. There's an excellent restaurant about a mile from here." She glanced quickly at his cane. "Do you drive?"

"I manage. I've rented a car with an automatic transmission. I brake with my left foot, and my right leg can handle the gas pedal."

"My, my, you even have ambidextrous feet." She smiled at him, then her gaze slid away. "I'll be right back."

Amnity Ames was a bit nervous, Tander mused, watching her stride quickly toward a back room. Good. He was certain that she was every bit as aware of him as a man as he was aware of her as a woman. And, oh, Lord, was he ever aware of her as a woman. He'd caught the aroma of the delicate cologne she was wearing, and had drawn the scent deep within him. It had intertwined with the heat gathering low in his body, and caused his heart to pound.

Ellis, he told himself, concentrate on the assignment. There were a lot of pieces missing from the puzzle, and he had questions to ask Amnity, with the hope she'd provide some of those pieces. He'd have to be on full alert, listening carefully, watching Amnity for any signs that she wasn't telling the truth. She would eventually trip herself up if she was caught in a tangle of lies, and he mustn't miss whatever clues she'd inadvertently give him.

Was Amnity helping her brother smuggle stolen diamonds?

No, dammit, she wasn't the type. She just didn't fit the mold of a criminal. Oh, who was he kidding. He'd met little gray-haired women who looked like somebody's grandmother, and who would have gladly slit his throat if given the chance. He had to remember that the jury in his mind was still out in regard to Amnity's guilt or innocence.

She walked back into the front area of the store wearing a royal-blue coat. Pressing some buttons on a panel, she extinguished the bright lights and turned on soft night-lights in their place.

He had to remain in a neutral zone, Tander told himself. He had to think only of the assignment during dinner. He'd do it. Somehow.

The restaurant was fashioned as a road-house during the colonial era in Virginia, with some amenities added for present-day comfort. The tables were made of wooden planks, sanded smooth, then varnished to a high sheen. Instead of wooden benches, captain's chairs with padded cushions welcomed the diners. Candles encased in sparkling hurricane lamps sat in the center of each table. The waitresses' costumes of long cotton dresses, white ruffled, aprons, and perky white dust caps added yet another authentic-looking touch to the atmosphere.

Amnity and Tander were shown to a table for two.

"Nice place," Tander said, glancing around. The room was aglow with soft candlelight, and the murmur of voices and clink of dishes was unobtrusive. "I wonder if Thomas Jefferson will pop in?"

Amnity smiled. "He just might. This restaurant always makes me feel as though I've been transported back in time. There's so much history in Virginia. I never get tired of visiting the various tourist attractions."

"Have you lived here long?" Five years, according to the report he'd read. She'd opened the Crazy Quilt after her father had died in prison.

"Five years," she said. "My father passed away then—my mother had died when I was eight—and I decided to start fresh in a new location. I've never been sorry."

"Do you have any other family?" Would she mention Andrew?

"I have an older brother named Andrew."

She paused. "I haven't seen or heard from him in over two years. He's a vagabond, a roamer, and I never know where he is."

So far, Tander thought, she was being very candid and up front. "That's too bad. I mean, that your brother doesn't keep in touch with you."

She fiddled with her spoon. "We don't have much in common, Andrew and I. We simply don't think alike, and run out of things to say to each other after ten minutes. I wish it were different, but . . ."

She shifted her gaze from the spoon to Tander.

"When . . . when Andrew and I were growing up, we were very close, especially after my mother died. Andrew was my hero, my knight in shining armor. I could go to him with any problem, big or small, and he'd find a way, somehow, to set things to rights. My father traveled a great deal, but when he came home, the three of us would have wonderful times together. It seemed that every day something special would happen, and he would bring us the most fabulous gifts, or take us on long vacations. Then, right before I graduated from high school . . ." She stopped, the memory, even ten years later, too painful to face. "You don't want to hear all this."

He took one of her hands in his. "Yes, I do. Go on with what you were saying."

"I don't usually talk about my personal life this way. I really don't know why I'm telling you all these things."

"Because I'm listening," he said quietly, looking directly into her eyes. "And I care."'

She stared at him for a long moment, then took a deep breath before she spoke again.

"Andrew chose a way of life," she continued, "that was difficult—no, impossible—for me to accept. I sometimes wonder if during these past two years he's gotten on the right track again, straightened himself out. I tell myself that's what his silence means, that he's putting his life back in proper order. He could do it, I know he could."

Ah, Amnity, Tander thought, tightening his hold on her hand.

"What about you, Tander? Do you have family here in Virginia?"

"No, my parents are retired and living in France." True. "My sister lives in Colorado with her husband." True. "I live on my boat, and go where my business takes me." True.

Her brows drew together in a slight frown. "Then you're a roamer, too, someone with a wanderlust spirit."

"Not completely. I just happen to be very fond of my yacht. I often stay in one spot for months at a stretch." True.

"What type of business are you in?"

"I'm an investment manager." Sort of true. It sounded as though he invested other people's money, when in actuality it was all his own. "I was working on putting a deal together here when I had my accident. I decided to stay put to recuperate, because I have a good rapport with my doctor. I trust him." That spiel was a bold-faced lie.

Amnity nodded slowly. "I can understand why you chose to stay. Trusting your doctor in circumstances like yours would be vitally important. In fact, trust is . . . well . . ." Her voice trailed off.

"What were you going to say?" he asked. "Trust is what?"

"Well, I feel that trust is imperative in any relationship. It's precious, like a treasure, and should never be treated lightly, or abused. Once trust is destroyed, it's difficult, if not impossible, to totally rebuild it."

"I see." He gently rubbed his thumb over her hand. "You know, sometimes we meet someone whom we trust from almost the moment we say hello. It's just there—that whatever it is that feels right clicks into place. Do you understand what I mean?"

Amnity stared into Tander's eyes. A strange warmth was spreading throughout her, she realized, a warmth that was very different from the heat of desire.

"Do you?" he asked.

"Yes," she whispered. "I understand what you're saying."

"Amnity—"

"Here's our dinner," she said, pulling her hand free. "Oh, it looks and smells heavenly. I'm famished."

Tander moved back and feigned interest as the waitress set their seafood platters in front of them. A knot had tightened in his gut as he'd listened to Amnity's softly spoken words, and eating no longer held any appeal.

He forced himself to take a bite of the flaky white fish, nodded in approval, and shoveled in a forkful of baked potato.

Trust, he mused. What would his lies do to any trust he managed to build between Amnity and himself? He didn't know. But one thing was for damn sure—Amnity Ames was innocent.

He knew it. He'd bank on it. That piece of the puzzle had been found, examined, and put securely in place.

He studied her as she ate, the candlelight casting a rosy glow over her. Her dark hair shone like silk, her skin appeared so soft, beckoning to his fingers to caress her cheeks, her lips.

"Aren't you hungry, Tander?" she asked, glancing at his plate, then meeting his gaze.

"What? Oh, sure." He took another bite of fish. "Great food, delicious."

"It certainly is." She reached for a biscuit from the cloth-lined wicker basket. "You should try one of these. They're scrumptious."

"Okay." He placed a biscuit that he didn't want on the edge of his plate.

Speaking of truth, he thought dryly, it was time he faced a very startling fact. Amnity Ames had become extremely important to him. Perhaps it was because he knew so much about her before he met her; or because he admired the way she had built a secure life for herself out of the ashes of her destroyed family. Or maybe it was because of that touch of vulnerability in her. Or perhaps it was just because she had the most alluring eyes he'd ever seen. Whatever the reason, or reasons, he was feeling amazingly drawn to her, amazingly quickly.

All morning and afternoon, he hadn't been able to stop thinking about her. Then, when he'd walked into her shop and seen her looking both so poised and tentative, he'd know he'd been waiting for that moment the entire day.

Was he falling in love with Amnity Ames?

He narrowed his eyes, waiting for a feeling of horror, of let-me-out-of-here panic, to assault him. Waiting for his lifelong stand that he intended to remain as free as the wind to rise to the fore.

A slow smile crept onto his lips. Well, well, well, he thought. Obviously, none of the things he was waiting for were going to show up, rap him on the head, and tell him to get his act together. There was a clear, uncluttered path between him and Amnity, between him and discovering just what these new, growing feelings for her meant.

Nothing in the way . . . except the lies.

Amnity buttered a small piece of biscuit and popped it into her mouth. She deserved an Academy Award for her performance, she decided. She was inhaling her dinner like a woman who hadn't eaten in days. The food tasted like sawdust, which turned into bricks in her stomach, landing there with a thud.

Her brilliant plan wasn't working!

Removing Tander from the Crazy Quilt and plopping him into an environment of other couples was doing nothing to diminish his vibrant masculinity. Every man in the restaurant she'd glanced at paled in comparison to Tander.

And what the candlelight did for his rugged, tanned features and amber-flecked eyes wasn't fair.

And the path her wayward thoughts took her down each time his sensual lips closed around his fork was shameful.

And the tempo of her racing heart and the heat of the desire churning low within her were increasing with every tick of the clock.

This was so frightening, she thought anxiously. Although she'd certainly enjoyed having dinner with other men, spending any time at all with Tander went way beyond enjoyable. It was downright intoxicating. She couldn't believe she'd told him even a little about her father and Andrew, her deeply held hope that Andrew had gotten his life together. Yet it had felt so comforting to share with Tander, to *trust* him with her inner feelings. Oh, no, she thought, she didn't want any of the reactions she was having to Tander. She was going to finish her dinner and end this outing with him pronto.

She had to put as much distance as she could between herself and Tander Ellis.

Three

On the deck of his yacht, Tander sank onto a padded bench, decided it was too cold, and went below to the large lounge. He tossed the needlepoint kit onto the small bar, then poured himself a stiff drink.

He'd been hustled, he thought incredulously. Tander Ellis, woman-charmer extraordinaire of the Western hemisphere, had been outmaneuvered by one Miss Amnity Elizabeth Ames.

After a dessert of cheesecake and coffee, a brightly smiling Amnity had suddenly announced that it was much later than she'd thought, and before Tander knew what hit him, they were driving back to the Crazy Quilt.

Tander shook his head and took a deep swallow of liquor.

Then, he remembered dismally, Amnity had stated breezily that there was no reason for him to park. She'd just hop into her own car and be home in twenty minutes. She'd enjoyed the delicious dinner ever so much, thanks again, and good night, Tander.

With that, she was gone. Tander slammed the glass down onto the bar.

As an agent on assignment, he thought, he'd blown it. As a man in the company of the woman who was evoking powerful emotions he'd never felt before, he'd *really* blown it.

He wanted to pull Amnity into his arms, fit her slender, soft body to the contours of his hard body, and kiss her luscious lips, which had been tantalizing him, inviting him to do just that through the entire meal.

He sat down on one of the sofas, then got up again and began to pace the floor. He was edgy, he realized, wired as tight as a drum.

Well, who wouldn't be, he asked himself, when entertaining, for the first time in his life, the possibility that he might be falling in love?

He hadn't planned on falling in love, had

viewed marriage and commitment as not in the cards for him. But it had become, he now realized, nothing more than habit, rather than conviction, to state over the years that he intended to remain as free as a bird.

But, by damn, if old Cupid had gotten off his butt and decided that Tander Ellis was the next in line to take the fall, it was fine with him.

More than fine.

After seeing the happiness shared by his friends Vince and Katha, and Declan and Joy, he was ready for his slice of that kind of pie. He was going to discover exactly how he felt about Amnity Ames.

If the lady in question would stand still for two seconds!

She was so wary, so obviously intent on ignoring her attraction to him. Well, nice try, Amnity, he told her silently, but give it up. When Tander Ellis made up his mind about something, it should be considered a *fait accompli.*

But what about the tower of lies he was building? No, he decided, he wasn't going to worry about that now.

He left the lounge and strode down the corridor to his bedroom. Sleep would rejuvenate his mind and body. Tomorrow was another day. And tomorrow Tander Ellis was taking charge.

"Amnity isn't here," the plump older woman said.

"What?" Tander asked. He'd worked on his rainbow until ten that morning, then driven to the Crazy Quilt. His plan had been to tell Amnity that he'd broken his needle and needed to buy another one. So what did he find? A grandmother type who was casually informing him that Amnity wasn't there. Well, where in the hell was she? "Where is she?"

"Oh, she could be anywhere," the grandmother said. "She phoned me early this morning and asked me to come in. I do this whenever she needs me, and it serves us both very well. I love being here, and Amnity gets a day off. She needs to take more of these breaks. Heaven knows how hard she works, how many hours she spends here, the dear girl. May I be of assistance to you, young man?"

Ooze charm, Ellis, Tander told himself. Turn it on full force. "Well, Grandma," he said, giving her his best and most charming smile. "May I call you Grandma? You remind me of my dear departed grandmother."

His grandmother, he thought wryly, smoked

a pipe and swore like a trooper while she drank whiskey straight up. She'd slug him for insinuating that she was dear and departed. Oh, well.

"Of course you may call me Grandma," the grandmother said. "That's really rather sweet. My grandchildren live in San Francisco, and I do miss them terribly. Now, then, how can I help you?"

Lord, he was good, Tander thought smugly. When he turned on the old charm, there was no stopping him. This was going to be a piece of cake.

"You see, Grandma," he said, his dazzling smile at one hundred watts, "my reasons for wanting to talk to Amnity are personal. They have nothing to do with the Crazy Quilt, if you get my drift. It's me, the man, wishing to speak with the lovely Amnity. So, if you'd be so kind as to tell me where she lives, I'll be on my way over there to check if she's home. I'll be forever in your debt, Grandma."

Five minutes later, Tander was driving back to the yacht, muttering every expletive he knew, plus the Italian ones he'd learned from Vince.

He had to retrace his steps and look up Amnity's address in the file he had on her on the yacht. The telephone book in the booth he'd stopped at had produced nothing.

And that grandma? Hell, she was tougher than the Gestapo. She'd issued a flat no to his request for Amnity's address, folded her arms, pursed her lips, and that had been that. There'd been no budging her.

They sure didn't make grandmothers the way they used to, he thought sullenly. His own grandmother being at the top of the weird list.

"You're losing your touch, Ellis," he said to his reflection in the rearview mirror, then pressed harder on the gas pedal.

One speeding ticket and two hours later, Tander knocked on the door of a small cottage, set back from the road and surrounded by tall trees. His mood was as dark as the gathering storm clouds in the winter sky. He knocked again, then leaned on his cane.

Amnity frowned as she heard one knock, then another, at the front door. She rested the mop against the counter and tiptoed across the wet kitchen floor, her bare toes squeaking on the shiny tile. A rumble from her stomach reminded her she'd had nothing to eat since dawn except a piece of toast and two cups of coffee.

She crossed the small living room, deciding she liked the new furniture arrangement she'd invented as part of her extensive cleaning binge. The scrubbing-and-rubbing spree of the cottage was her method of dealing with frazzled nerves and excess energy caused by tension. Tension and frazzled nerves caused by one Mr. Tander Ellis.

Her spit-and-shine therapy had held her in good stead during high-stress times in the past. By the end of several hours of cleaning, she'd be fit as a fiddle, and Tander would no longer hover stubbornly in her mental vision.

She opened the door and stared wide-eyed at a smiling Tander. Oh, how sad, she thought giddily, she'd lost her mind. She was experiencing a mirage. She could actually see Tander standing in front of her, which was, of course, impossible.

"Hello, Amnity," he said.

"Oh, Lord." One hand flew to her forehead. "It speaks."

Tander's smile faded. "What?"

Amnity blinked, blinked again, then planted her hands on her hips. "You're really here. What are you doing here? How did you know where I lived? Grace wouldn't give anyone my address. You can't be here."

"Could you run that by me a little slower?" Damn, she looked great, he thought. She had adorable toes, and legs, in faded jeans, that went on forever. She was wearing a baggy gray sweatshirt that said PROPERTY OF THE WHITE HOUSE on the front, and as far as he could tell, she hadn't bothered to put on any makeup. Here was yet another side to Amnity. Sensational. "Forget that. May I come in?"

"No. Absolutely not." She sighed. "That was rude, and I'm not a rude person." She stepped back. "Yes, come in . . . for a moment. What are you doing here?"

Tander limped into the room and glanced around as Amnity shut the door behind him.

Very nice, he decided. The cottage was cozy, with a puffy flowered sofa and chairs, and a multitude of throw pillows lining the sofa. An afghan was folded over the back of a rocking chair that sat by the small fireplace.

He was certain Amnity had made the pillows and afghan, as well as the framed samplers on the walls. It was an inviting little place, and suited her due to the special touches she'd added.

"I really like what you've done here," he said, turning to face her.

"Thank you," she mumbled. Oh, Tander, go away. He was ruining everything, didn't he know that? She needed to be alone, to work herself into a state of limp exhaustion so that she could be free of him, of his image, the remembrance of his smile, his compelling eyes and magnificent body. Oh, why was he here? "Why are you here, Tander?"

"I wanted to see you," he said quietly.

She wrapped her arms around her waist. "Why? Are you still having problems with your rainbow?"

"No, the needlepoint is coming along fine. I just have to remember always to use my right hand. I'm not here because of my rainbow."

"How did you know where I lived?"

"I have a friend who works for the county." Chalk up another lie for Tander Ellis. "He looked up your address on the tax rolls."

"That's illegal."

He smiled slightly. "It's innovative. The grandmother at your store can keep secrets better than the CIA. I wasn't even sure you'd be home, but . . . Amnity, I really wanted to see you."

She peered down at her bare toes, curling them into the tan carpet. "Well, I'm very busy right now. I'm cleaning my house, every single inch of it. I don't have time to chat today."

"Amnity, look at me."

"No." She sounded about four years old, but she didn't care. He had to leave. Now.

"Okay, I'll talk to the top of your head. You

know, and I know, that something is happening between us."

Her head popped up. "There is nothing happening between us, Tander Ellis. Don't be absurd. Now, if you'll excuse me . . ."

"No, I won't excuse you. Your spring cleaning, or winter cleaning, or whatever the hell it is that you're doing, can wait. This is important."

"Now *you're* being rude."

"Well, pardon me all to hell and back," he said, his volume rising. "There *is* something happening between us, something different, special, and I, for one, want to know exactly what it is."

"Well, I, for one, don't give diddly-squat *what* it is," she said, just as loudly.

"Ah-ha! So you admit that there *is* something happening here."

"No, I didn't say that. I simply meant that if there were, I wouldn't care because . . . But there isn't, so it's a moot point. Therefore—"

"Oh, hell. This conversation is nuts. I've had enough of this garbage."

He closed the distance between them, vaguely aware that he'd forgotten to lean on the cane. He slipped his free hand to the nape of her neck, lowered his head, and kissed her.

Oh, no, Amnity thought desperately. He couldn't, shouldn't do this. He . . . Yes, yes,

he could, and should, and *was* doing this.
Oh, Tander.

Her eyes closed as her arms floated up to
encircle his neck. She parted her lips as his
insistent tongue urged her to do, and returned his heated kiss passionately.

He tasted so good, and felt so good, and
desire was pulsing deep within her. She'd
waited a lifetime for this kiss, this man. She
wouldn't think about it now. She would only
savor, and want, and need, Tander Ellis.

Sensations exploded within Tander like a
flash fire bursting into flames that were instantly out of control. He dropped the cane
and gathered Amnity close to his throbbing
body, aching with desire for her.

Never, he thought hazily, had there been a
kiss like this one. Never before had he been
so consumed by a tide of passion burning
within him. This kiss was all and more than
he'd imagined it could be.

This was Amnity.

He lifted his head to take a quick, raspy
breath, then claimed her mouth again, drink-
ing in her sweet nectar, inhaling her delicate
aroma, memorizing the feel of her soft curves
nestled to his hard body.

This was Amnity.

And this was love.

Mingling with the heat of his arousal were

the greatest joy, and peace, and sense of completeness that he had ever known.

He raised his head again, his breathing rough. Reluctantly, he eased her away from his hungry body, and immediately missed the feel of her. Cradling her face in his hands, he nearly groaned when he saw smoky desire clouding her eyes.

"Amnity," he murmured, his voice hoarse with passion and emotion.

Amnity tore her gaze from him as sudden, unexpected tears filled her eyes. For a few ecstatic, stolen minutes she'd simply been herself, a woman, with no past, no present, no future. She'd been captured in the now, in a place that held only herself and Tander, and a desire that had swept away all of her fears.

But reality had returned, forcing her to remember all that had happened in the past. And reality held her heart in a fist of iron. Reality declared that she must remain alone, for to trust and love brought only the painful heartache of betrayal.

Two tears slid down her cheeks.

"Amnity," Tander whispered, "don't cry." He caught her tears with his thumbs, then gently stroked her cheeks. "You look so sad, and it's ripping me up. Don't be sorry about this. It's fantastic, can't you see that? There's something unbelievably beautiful happening between us." He loved her. Oh, yes, he loved her. But he knew she wasn't ready to hear those words yet. "Hey, everything is fine, really great."

"No," she said, stepping back. He dropped his hands from her face. "I can't lie to you, Tander. Truth is too important to me to lie to you." She drew in an unsteady breath, and a painful knot twisted in Tander's gut. "Those kisses were . . . wonderful. I felt so special, so . . . But I can't, won't, go further. Whatever this is between us doesn't matter, because I don't want it. Please, Tander, just go. Leave me alone."

"No."

"Aren't you listening to me?"

"No." He paused. "Well, yes, I'm listening, but I can't just shrug this off and go on my merry way. This is too important. I won't push you or rush you, but I'm sure as hell not walking out of your life."

"Yes, you are," she said, wrapping her hands around her elbows in a protective gesture.

"No, Amnity, I'm not."

"Dammit, Tander Ellis!" she yelled, "I'm half of whatever this is. I have a voice in this. Do you understand?"

"Sure. I hear your voice. Your half obviously hasn't caught up with my half, but I'll wait for you. No problem. I'm a patient man."

"You," she said, narrowing her eyes, "are an infuriating man. You're very accustomed, I imagine, to having things go entirely your way when it comes to women. Well, not this time, bub. It takes two to . . . to . . ."

"Tango?" he suggested, raising his eyebrows.

She pointed to the door. "Go!"

Thunder rumbled in the distance.

"Go?" he repeated. "It's about to rain out there."

"You won't melt."

He bent down and picked up the discarded cane, then leaned on it, hating the lie of his actions. He looked at Amnity again, and his voice was low and serious when he spoke.

"I'll go . . . for now, because I said I wouldn't rush you. I'll leave, but the essence of what we shared in this room will still be here." He glanced around, as though he could see a tangible entity, then met her gaze once more. "You can toss me out . . . for now, but what will you do with the memories, with the truth of what's happening between us?"

"Tander, don't," she said, tears nearly choking off her voice. "Just don't. Please."

He gazed at her for a long moment, wishing he knew how to reach beyond her pain to her heart. "I'm leaving because I don't want to be the cause of your tears."

The heavens opened, and rain began to beat down on the roof of the cottage.

"But I can't walk out of your life forever," he went on, "because nothing like this, like you, has ever happened to me before. I . . ." *I love you, Amnity Ames.* "Hear the rain? Remember that sometimes there's a rainbow after the storm. It's time for you to believe in wishes on rainbows again." He started toward the door, not limping as badly as he knew he should. "Think about it." He left the cottage, closing the door quietly behind him.

Amnity stood motionless, willing her tears to stop flowing and her body to cease its trembling. The sound of the rain beat against her mind, along with Tander's parting words.

"Wishes on rainbows," she whispered. No, she couldn't allow herself to step back into a world that held false promises, even if that world was beckoning to her, urging her to emerge from within her protective walls and move into Tander's embrace. She couldn't because her fear was greater than the heated desire for Tander still pulsing deep within her.

She covered her face with her hands, bowed her head, and wept.

• • •

When Tander returned to the yacht, he immediately shed his cold, rain-soaked clothes and stood under a hot shower. The message that had beaten against his mind as steadily as the rain against his body continued to repeat itself.

He was in love with Amnity Ames.

As he dried with a large royal-blue towel, then dressed in black cords and a green sweater, he knew he was smiling. Actually, he was grinning like a fool, but he didn't care.

He was in love, by damn!

Lord, it was good. No, it was great, fantastic. He'd buy a big house, here in Virginia, or in California, or wherever Amnity wanted. A big house with a big yard for the children to play in.

Yes, he and Amnity would have a baby. As many babies as she wanted. It would be wonderful watching her grow big with the child they'd created from beautiful, exquisite lovemaking.

They'd decorate the nursery together. Amnity would make beautiful needlepoint designs for the walls, and she'd probably sew a bunch of little clothes, and—

Whoa, an inner voice said. Hold it, Ellis.

He sat down on the bed and stared blindly at the far wall.

He was getting way ahead of himself. He was in love, but Amnity sure as hell wasn't. She was fighting her feelings for him every inch of the way, and he'd bet his entire checking account that her lousy father and brother were at the bottom of that. Not good.

And he was adding to the distance between them with every lie he told her. Not good at all.

The telephone rang, jolting Tander from his rambling thoughts. He snatched the receiver up.

"Ellis."

"Vince. How are you, Tander?"

In love. "Fine."

"Good. Listen, I have some news. Hank Murphy just called from Washington. Andrew Ames has dropped out of sight. None of the diamonds stolen in Greece have surfaced among the fences, and now Andrew is nowhere to be found. I figure he's headed for this country, somehow. Probably on a cargo ship, if he's still as smart as he's been in the past. He wouldn't risk commercial transportation. I also think he's too bright to have the diamonds with him."

"Meaning?"

"He's arranged to have them smuggled in, and is on his way to collect them when they arrive."

"Makes sense."

"Tander, we can't ignore the fact that our informant heard Amnity Ames's name mentioned, as well as the name of her shop. You've got to find out if Amnity is expecting any kind of shipment from overseas, specifically Greece."

"Yeah, well . . ." He ran his hand over the back of his neck. "Look, Vince, Amnity isn't in on this deal with Andrew. If the diamonds *are* being shipped to her store, she's an innocent pawn."

Vince was silent for a long moment. "You sound very certain of that," he said finally.

"I am."

"Why?"

"Dammit, Santini, don't you trust my judgment, my instincts? I'm telling you that Amnity isn't working with her brother. There was a time when the way I called it was good enough for you."

"Okay, okay, take it easy." Vince paused again. "Tander, is there something you're not telling me? I get the feeling that . . . Holy hell, Ellis. Are you . . . Tander, are you in love with Amnity Ames?"

"Why in the hell would you think that?"

"It fits, that's all. You usually operate on the theory that everyone is guilty until you've had plenty of time to decide who's innocent.

For you to be so adamant so quickly about Amnity not being involved in this tells me a whole helluva lot. Come on, Tander, spill it."

Tander drew a deep breath and let it out slowly. "Okay. I love her, all right? I'm in love with Amnity. And unlike some dumb yo-yo I know, I'm not fighting my feelings. I love her, I'm glad—to say the least—that I do, and that's that. The bottom line, Santini, is that Amnity is not Andrew's partner in this stolen-diamond deal. And, no, my judgment isn't clouded by my feelings for Amnity, which was probably your next thought."

"Bingo."

"You're just going to have to trust me on this, Vince."

"I've trusted you with my life in the past, but, hell, Tander, you've never been in love before. Love can scramble a guy's brain. Lord, Tander Ellis in love. I never thought I'd hear those words coming from you. Of course, I never expected to hear myself say them, either. Under different circumstances, I'd break out the champagne. As it stands, you're making me nervous."

"Thanks a lot. Your faith in me is over-whelming."

"I know the power of a woman once you've fallen in love with her. Love is potent stuff, Tander."

"Believe me, I realize that. But, Vince, I'm positive that Amnity is innocent. Don't give me the third degree about how I know, just trust me. Either this is my assignment or it isn't. I do it my way or I don't do it. Your ball, Santini."

Again Vince was silent for a long moment. "Your ball, your game," he said quietly. "Play it as you see it. Keep in touch."

"Thanks, Vince."

"Watch your back. And, Tander? Watch your heart. If you're wrong about . . . No, forget it. I'll let you know if I get any more info. See ya."

"Yeah, see ya," Tander said, then slowly replaced the receiver.

Vince Santini hung up, then dragged both hands down his face. He stared up at the ceiling for a long moment, then shook his head.

"Oh, hell," he muttered.

Early the next morning, Tander sat in his car on a side street that gave him a clear view of Amnity's cottage. He'd decided, somewhere in the middle of his nearly sleepless night, that he wasn't running the risk of going to the Crazy Quilt and finding the Gestapo grandmother on duty.

Time, he knew, was one of his enemies. Andrew was making his move, and Tander was nowhere near gaining Amnity's trust. Another fierce enemy was the lies he was scattering like shards of broken glass on the path between Amnity and himself.

He sat staring at her front door for nearly an hour, until at last it opened and she emerged.

Good morning, my love, he whispered silently. He wanted to run across that street, haul her into his arms, and kiss her for three hours. Eight hours. Hell, forever.

She got into her car and drove away. Tander followed.

Her destination, he soon discovered, was a small restaurant. She'd walked halfway across the parking lot when she stopped and waved to a woman driving in.

"Breakfast with a girlfriend," Tander muttered. "Okay, ladies, you're about to have company."

"You look awful," Amnity's best friend, Beth Wilson, told her. "Totally exhausted."

Amnity smiled at the attractive blonde and slipped off her coat, allowing it to pool behind her in the booth. "You're wonderful for my ego, Beth. Last week you said I looked terrific."

"That was last week. Today, you look exhausted. Has it been busy at the Crazy Quilt?"

"Yes, very busy, but I'm tired because I cleaned my house from top to bottom yesterday."

"Uh-oh," Beth said, leaning her elbows on the table. "Tell all. What's bothering you, Amnity? You only do your cleaning marathons when you've got something heavy on your mind."

"You know me too well."

"What are best friends for?"

The waitress appeared beside their table. "Ready to order?"

"Definitely," Beth said. "I'm starving."

Orders were placed, coffee cups filled, then Beth watched the waitress walk away.

"Alone at last," she said. "Now, Amnity, confess. What's wrong?" She stared up at the ceiling. "Please let it be a man. My prayers will be answered if there's a gorgeous hunk of stuff in Amnity Ames's life . . . and bed."

"Beth, for heaven's sake. I—" Her eyes widened as she looked beyond Beth to the door of the restaurant. "Oh, my gosh, how did he . . . ?" She quickly redirected her attention to Beth, leaning toward her. "Just go along with me, okay?"

"What?"

"Shh. Listen. He refuses to get the message that I'm not interested in . . . I think maybe I'm just a challenge to him, because he's not used to having women who . . . So, I'm changing my strategy. I'm going to scare the bejeebers out of him, and he'll hightail it out of my life."

"Huh?"

"Shh." She straightened in the booth and smiled. "Tander. My, my, what a surprise."

Tander limped to their table. "Yes, it is," he said, smiling. "I was up early and decided to go out for breakfast."

"Beth," Amnity said, "this is Tander Ellis. Tander, this is Beth Wilson, my best friend and my attorney."

"Hello, Tander," Beth said pleasantly, her gaze sweeping over him. She glanced at Amnity, then looked back at Tander. "It's delightful to meet you."

"The pleasure is mine," he said. "Well, I don't want to intrude. I'll find a table."

Amnity scooped up her coat and slid closer to the wall, then patted the space next to her in the booth.

"Don't be silly, Tander," she said, smiling ever so sweetly. "Why should you be way over there, when you could be right next to me here? There are no secrets between Beth and myself. I was just tellling her all about you. Isn't that right, Beth?"

"Oh, right, right," Beth said. "I feel as though I know you, Tander." She cleared her throat. "Yes, indeed. Yes."

Tander narrowed his eyes, gazing intently at Amnity. "Is that a fact? Interesting." And confusing. What in the hell was Amnity up to? he wondered.

She patted the seat again. "Don't you want to sit your little old self right down here next to little old me?"

"Good Lord," Beth muttered under her breath.

"You bet I do," Tander said. "I wouldn't miss this breakfast for the world."

Four

This was not, Amnity decided, a good idea.

She draped her coat over the back of the booth as Tander slid in next to her. The waitress appeared instantly, smiling brightly, and took Tander's order for waffles. Coffee cups were tended to, then the still-smiling waitress hurried away.

Now, there they were, Amnity thought dismally, herself and Tander, squeezed together like two peas in a pod. The heat from Tander's leg that was pressed against hers was incredible. The warmth was traveling through her entire body like insistent, tingling fingers; swirling low within her, then sweeping upward to dance across her breasts, which were feeling strangely heavy and achy. No, this had definitely not been a good idea.

"So," Tander said to Beth, "you're an attorney. Do you specialize?"

"Not really," Beth said. "I handle a little bit of everything. I find that more challenging. Amnity and I met five years ago, when I acted in her behalf to negotiate the lease for the building housing the Crazy Quilt. Have you known Amnity long, Tander?" She stiffened slightly. "What I mean is, Amnity has told me all about you, but I don't seem to remember just when you two met."

Tander hid his smile. Perry Mason Beth hadn't heard of him until he'd shown up in the restaurant two minutes ago.

"Well," he said, "if you were charting it on a calendar, I'd guess you could say I haven't known Amnity very long. But time, Beth, isn't important in matters of the heart." He smiled at Amnity, who was staring at him rather blankly, then looked at Beth again. "Get the drift?"

Smiling dreamily, Beth plunked one elbow on the table and rested her chin in her hand. "Oh, yes, I understand completely. That's marvelous, and so romantic. I can't tell you how delighted I am that Amnity has found— Ow!" She jerked suddenly.

"Oh, dear," Amnity said, "did I kick you,

Beth? I'm so very sorry. It's a tad crowded under the table. Ah, here's our breakfast. I've got to eat and run. I have a million things to do at the store before I open."

"You do?" Tander said, as his waffles were set in front of him. "Like what?"

She straightened the plate containing her omelet. "Dust. I have to dust."

"Amnity's really into cleaning," Tander said, dribbling syrup over his waffles. "She was scrubbing her cottage yesterday from stem to stern."

"You were there while she was cleaning?" Beth asked.

"Well, sure. But because of my bum knee, I wasn't much help. I finally just got out of her way, as much as I hated to leave. Right, Amnity?"

"No," she said. I mean, yes, you left, but . . ." Darn it, he was making it sound as if they'd been a cozy couple cleaning cobwebs together. Even his tone of foice gave obvious sexual connotations to his having been at her cottage. Of course, he *had* kissed her until she couldn't breathe and . . . No, she wasn't thinking about that. She'd spent half the night reliving those kisses. "Pass the salt, please."

Tander picked up the saltshaker and held it toward her. As she wrapped her fingers around it, he lifted his other hand to sand-wich hers and the saltshaker between his. She stared at him in surprise.

"Excuse me, Beth," he said, his gaze riv-eted on Amnity, "but I really need to say good morning to Amnity properly."

"Oh, be my guest," Beth said breezily. "Just pretend I'm not here."

Amnity's eyes widened as Tander leaned toward her.

"Good morning," he murmured huskily. "I can't tell you how much your warm welcome this morning means to me."

"But I—"

"So, good morning, my love," he added, and he kissed her.

He couldn't kiss her in a restaurant! Amnity screamed silently. But he was, and it was heaven, and it was—Drat, it was over.

She blinked and nearly dropped the salt into her coffee cup when Tander released her hand. Her heart was racing, the heat within her had reached the boiling point, and her face was warm with the flush of arousal.

She busied herself sprinkling salt on her omelet. *Good morning, my love.* His voice echoed in her heart and mind. My love . . . my love. She'd never been anyone's love be-fore. *My love.* What would it be like to escape from the past, to give all of herself to Tander Ellis, and have him love her for eternity?

"You're putting an awful lot of salt on that omelet," Tander said.

"What? Oh." She thudded the saltshaker onto the table.

"By the way, Amnity," Beth said, "I've taken care of those papers with customs. They have their check in New York, and your orders will be delivered to the Crazy Quilt with no hassle, as usual."

Warning bells went off in Tander's head, and he pulled his thoughts from Amnity and the sensational kiss they'd just shared. There was, he reminded himself, an assignment in the works. He wanted to do nothing more than concentrate on Amnity and the fact that he was in love with her, but . . .

"Customs?" he said. "I didn't realize you get some of your supplies from overseas, Amnity."

"I don't on a regular basis." She took a bite of the omelet and nearly choked from the overabundance of salt. She gulped down some coffee. "When I do, Beth handles all of the paperwork."

"I see," Tander said pleasantly. "So what exotic stuff are you getting from where this time?" Not Greece. For godsake, not Greece. If Andrew had involved Amnity in the diamond smuggling, he was going to find that scum and take him apart.

"What's cleared to come in, Beth?" Amnity asked.

Thank goodness, Amnity thought, they were all just chatting like normal people having breakfast. Not that she could eat her omelet, because she'd killed it with the salt, but there was a glimmer of hope that she could survive being so close to Tander without making a complete fool of herself.

Her plan had royally backfired, she admitted. She'd put it into action on impulse, but Tander wasn't intimidated one iota by her "Don't you want to sit by little old me?" routine. He hadn't cut and run. He'd sat by little old her and kissed her senseless. And she was a wreck.

"Let's see," Beth said. "There's that silk embroidery thread from Spain, the linen is in from Ireland, and . . ." She squinted, deep in thought.

And? Tander mentally prompted. So far, so good. Say that that's all, Beth. He wanted her to announce that there was nothing else arriving from overseas.

"What about my present to myself?" Amnity asked. "Has it reached New York?"

Every muscle in Tander's body tightened.

Beth snapped her fingers. "Yes, that's it. I knew I was forgetting something."

"Oh, wonderful," Amnity said, smiling

brightly. "When I saw it in the auction cata-
log, I managed to convince myself that I really deserved to have it. I can hardly wait to
see it."

"The suspense is too much to bear," Tander
said, hoping his voice sounded normal. "What
are you giving yourself as a special present,
Amnity?"

She turned to look at him, her eyes sparkling with excitement. "An antique crazy quilt.
It was part of an estate that was being auc-
tioned off. The owners were Americans who
retired over there, and the quilt was made in
this country at the turn of the century. It's
gorgeous . . . or at least it was in the bro-
chure. It's one of those unique padded crazy
quilts that took months and months of te-
dious work to complete. I had an auction
house here place my bid for me, and I got it.
Oh, I hope it doesn't take forever for it to
arrive from New York."

Beth laughed. "Patience, Miss Ames. You're
like a kid on her birthday."

Americans who retired over there, Tander
thought. Over where? He had to ask but,
dammit, at that moment he just didn't want
to know.

"Have you ever seen a crazy quilt, Tander?"
Amnity went on. "Each one is different, made
from scraps of material that hold special

meaning and memories. There's no set pattern to follow when sewing the pieces together. The padded quilts have cotton batting stuffed between the layers every few inches to give added character. The one I'm getting has bright, cheerful colors. Oh, I'm so eager to actually see it."

"What—" He stopped to clear his throat. "What country is the quilt coming in from?"

"Greece," Amnity said. "Can you imagine the stories that quilt could tell if it could talk? It's so old, and it's traveled . . ."

Amnity's exuberant chatter was drowned out by the roaring in Tander's ears.

Greece!

Damn that Andrew Ames straight to hell! He was actually going to do it. Ames was using his own sister as a means to smuggle stolen diamonds into the country.

Those pieces of the puzzle fit. The informant in Greece had overheard Amnity's name and "the crazy quilt." The latter, apparently, had a double meaning. It wasn't only Amnity's store, but also the crazy quilt she was expecting from Greece.

Andrew, the louse, must be cackling in glee over his good fortune at discovering that his sister had a quilt being shipped to the United States.

Tander narrowed his eyes. Oh, yes, he was

looking forward to coming face-to-face with Andrew Ames. The scum thought he was home free by using Amnity. Where Andrew had made his mistake was that Amnity Ames was the woman Tander Ellis loved.

"Tander?" Amnity asked. "What's wrong? You suddenly look . . . I don't know . . . angry."

He slid one arm across her shoulders and kissed her on the forehead. "My knee is throbbing. You said yourself that it's a bit crowded under this table. I need to take a walk and give the knee a little workout." Soon, he thought. Soon there would be no more need for lies. Soon he'd be able to tell Amnity how he truly felt about her. She'd understand about his deception. She just had to. "I'm going to take off for now. I'll see you at the store later, or give you a call."

He dropped a quick, hard kiss on her lips, then picked up the check, replacing it with a couple of bills for the waitress's tip.

"Breakfast is on me," he said, sliding out of the booth. "After all, I crashed your party. Great meeting you, Beth. I'll talk to you later, Amnity."

"But . . ." Amnity started.

" 'Bye for now," he said, and limped away.

Amnity watched him as he stopped at the front counter to pay the check, then disappeared out the door. She switched her gaze to a smiling Beth.

"Well, well," Beth said, "you're certainly full of surprises. Tander is a gorgeous man, Amnity. Not only that, but I like him as a person. *And* he's obviously nuts about you. Yes, indeed, your Tander is something."

"He isn't mine," Amnity said quietly.

Beth's smile faded. "Oh, Amnity, we've been friends for so long. I know how terribly hurt you were by what your father and brother did, but you've got to look to the future. Men like Tander don't come along every day of the week. You care for him. It shows on your face, in your eyes. You're not going to deny it, are you?"

Amnity sighed. "No. I *do* care for Tander. From the moment I first saw him, I felt different, strange, excited, and . . ."

"And?" Beth asked, leaning toward her.

"And frightened."

"Amnity, don't let ghosts stand between you and Tander. It's your turn for some happiness."

"I'm happy," Amnity said, sitting up straighter. "I have the Crazy Quilt and a few good friends. I date several interesting men. Yes, Tander is special, he makes me feel . . . But I won't fall in love with him, Beth, because I don't want to. I don't want a serious relationship with Tander Ellis. And that, as they say, is that."

"Sweetie," Beth said, smiling pleasantly, "all I have to say is, bull."

"A padded crazy quilt," Vince said. "Yep, it would work. Andrew is a clever boy."

Tander gripped the telephone so tightly, his knuckles turned white. "Andrew Ames is operating on borrowed time."

"Easy, Tander. He'll scream from there to Washington if you rough him up."

Tander took a deep breath, then let it out slowly, forcing some of the tension to ebb from his coiled muscles. "Okay, I hear you."

"Good. Now then, let's see what we have. I don't think Andrew would risk trying to snatch the quilt while it's being shuffled around in New York. Why should he? He knows exactly where it's going. He'll just wait until it arrives at Amnity's store, then go in and get it."

Tander clenched his jaw until his teeth ached. "And I'll be the welcoming committee for him."

"Bingo. I guess I don't have to tell you that Amnity's safety is priority one. You've said she's not involved in this scam, so that makes her an innocent citizen caught in the middle." Vince paused. "Tander, do you think there's a chance Amnity would cooperate in helping to nab her own brother?"

"What do you mean?"

"It's a lot easier to stake out a place if the owner has given you the key and says, 'Go for it.' When Andrew breaks into the shop to snatch the quilt, you grab him, and that's it, end of story."

"I'll have to think this through," Tander muttered, running his hand over the back of his neck.

"It would make it go a lot smoother. All right, that's it for now. I'll leave the decision to you as to what and when to tell Amnity. She's your lady, Tander. You'll know the best way to handle this."

"Oh, sure, right," Tander said dryly.

"Love is complicated, isn't it?" Vince said, chuckling. "Well, watch your back, because Andrew Ames is heading your way. You can bank on it. See ya, Tander."

"See ya," Tander said, then hung up. He leaned his head back on the top of the sofa and closed his eyes. "Damn."

Through the long hours of that day, Amnity thought about Tander. She continually replayed in her mind each moment she'd spent with him. Each precious, glorious moment.

Slowly, cautiously, she'd allowed him to enter her safe space, to inch his way emotionally closer and closer to her.

Each small step she'd taken with him had been a risk, yet she'd paid no heartbreaking penalty. She had, instead, reaped wondrous rewards. His smile, his voice, the gentle caring she saw in his eyes, had begun to fill the chilling emptiness within her.

Years ago, she had chanced an intimate relationship, knowing that although she cared for the man, she didn't love him as she should. She had hoped she'd feel safer that way, yet in the end had realized that intimacy without love was as bad as no love at all.

Tander, she knew, wouldn't settle for such a tentative commitment. He'd demand everything from a woman—and give everything in return. Maybe that was why she was finding him so irresistible.

Could she trust him, though? Or would he lie to her the way her father and brother had?

Restless and confused, she wandered through her momentarily empty store. She stopped in the needlepoint section and stared at a rainbow kit like the one that Tander was working. She traced the arc of the vibrant rainbow, the cellophane package crackling beneath her finger.

A soft smile crept onto her lips as she imagined Tander struggling to complete each tiny stitch. She could envision his tawny eyebrows knitted in a frown, an expression of deep concentration on his face.

Big, strong, masculine Tander Ellis was determined to conquer the complexities of needlepoint, and woe be to the person who heckled him during his efforts. Tander Ellis would complete his rainbow.

"And then," she whispered, "he can make wishes."

And he would, she knew, because Tander was a man who lived for today and the tomorrows yet to come.

And herself? She was a prisoner of her past, held captive behind high walls she'd constructed around her heart. The brilliant colors of a rainbow couldn't reach her where she hid in gloomy shadows. Even a man with the strength and determination of Tander couldn't break through her protective walls unless she allowed him to.

Tears filled Amnity's eyes once again. With trembling hands, she slid the rainbow kit free, then pressed it to her breasts, holding it tightly.

Shortly after six o'clock that evening, as

Tander drove to Amnity's cottage, he came to a very startling and disturbing conclusion: He did not understand women. To be more precise, he did not understand Amnity Ames.

After much thought, he'd deduced that Amnity's warm and almost too sweet greeting of him in the restaurant that morning had been an effort to jar him, perhaps get him to exit stage left from her life. He'd thrown her off-kilter by going along with her, and she had responded totally to his unexpected kiss.

But, he'd reasoned, when he considered how to approach her about dinner, she'd had all day to reinforce her protective walls. He had no intention of taking her out to eat only to be outmaneuvered by her again.

Therefore, he'd called her at the Crazy Quilt with the suggestion that he meet her at her cottage, and he would bring take-out Chinese for dinner. He'd been fully prepared to play on her sympathies, tell her that his knee was killing him and he needed to rest it as much as possible.

So, what happened? He'd got no further than take-out Chinese when she announced that the idea sounded lovely, she'd see him soon, and good-bye.

No, he reaffirmed, he did *not* understand his lady. But he sure as hell loved her. And he *did* understand himself. The lies he was continually telling Amnity were weighing heavily on his soul, and worsening whenever he pictured them as obstacles to winning her heart, her love, for all time.

Tonight, he vowed, he would tell her everything. He had to hope, and toss in a prayer or two, that she would accept his explanation of why he had initially deceived her.

And lurking in the shadows of his mind was the worry that Amnity still felt a sense of family loyalty toward Andrew. He knew she was clutching at a thread of hope that her brother had straightened out his life in the past two years.

This night, Tander knew, was more important than he had words to describe. The knot in his gut told him how nervous he was. He wanted to get to Amnity's, stuff her full of Chinese food, then sit her down and tell her the truth about his assignment . . . and her brother.

And then he'd tell her that he loved her with all that he was.

"You blow this, Ellis," he said to his reflection in the rearview mirror, "and I'll strangle you."

Amnity stood in front of the full-length mirror in her bedroom, staring at her image.

She looked strangely different, she decided. Her skin seemed to be glowing, and there was a soft warmth in her eyes that hadn't been there before.

She turned her head back and forth, watching her dark hair swing with the motion, then fall back into place. Even her hair appeared unusually shiny and silky.

The caftan she wore, she mused, was so pretty. It was soft, pale blue wool with a garden of pastel flowers she'd embroidered along the hem and edges of the wrist-length, flowing sleeves.

A knock sounded at the door.

"I'm coming," she called, and hurried out of the bedroom.

She opened the front door and smiled at Tander, her heart racing. He was wearing dark slacks with a pale blue sweater almost the exact shade of her caftan.

"Hello," she said, stepping back. "Please come in."

He limped into the room, carrying a large white sack. "You look sensational," he said, his gaze sweeping over her. "Really beautiful."

"Thank you. That food smells delicious. Why don't I spread it out on the table in the dining alcove while you set a match to the kindling in the fireplace? I'm hungry, and I'm sure you must be too. I'm glad you thought of this. I haven't had Chinese food in ages. What would you like to drink?"

"Whatever you're having." Was he imagining it, or was she talking a hundred miles an hour? Maybe he just thought she sounded nervous because *he* was so nervous.

She took the bag from him, then spun around and headed toward the table. After setting out the small white boxes, she moved back into the living room. Tander was sitting in front of the fireplace, his back to her, and she stood motionless, staring at him.

As the kindling caught, its flames leaping up around the logs she'd laid, she felt a strange warmth fill her. She closed her eyes to savor that warmth, and colors danced across the back of her lids. The colors of a rainbow.

She imagined the rainbow was arching over her, and Tander stood at one end, the beautiful colors pouring over him like an iridescent waterfall.

The warmth flowed through her, washing away the last chill of fear and loneliness that had encased her for so long.

She felt as though she were standing at the edge of Creation. She could no longer delay the decision she had to make, a decision that could change her life forever.

She drew a shaky breath and opened her eyes.

Tander was still there, staring into the fire. It was his warmth, she knew, that filled her, his warmth that gave her the strength to fling away her protective walls. She would risk all and everything for him, for she had no choice. She loved him. And that love was more powerful than the ghosts of her past.

He rose awkwardly, leaning on his cane, and turned to her. "Ready?" he asked.

She nodded, afraid that if she spoke, she would blurt out that she loved him.

They settled at the table and filled their plates with fried dumplings and sesame noodles and spicy beef with orange sauce.

As he took his first bite, Tander decided to keep the conversation casual during dinner. They'd chat about her store, the weather, whatever came to mind. But there seemed to be a strange tension in the air, an aura of—of sensuality. Amnity looked so beautiful, and somehow different. He couldn't put his finger on what it was, but . . . Hell, Ellis, he told himself. Eat a dumpling and say something brilliant about a recent movie or a good book.

"Amnity," he said, "I love you." Oh, Lord, he didn't say that!

Her head snapped up, her eyes wide and startled. "What?" He was telling her that he loved her? Right in the middle of the chop suey, Tander Ellis was declaring his love for her? How glorious! How wonderful! "Oh, Tander, I—"

"Damn," he interrupted, shaking his head. "I didn't mean to say that. Well, I did mean to say it, and I meant what I said, but I didn't mean to say it until after . . . I'm blowing this straight to hell."

"No. No, you're not." She smiled warmly at him. "Tander, I—I love you too. I never thought I'd say those words to any man, but I *am* saying them to you. I love you, Tander Ellis."

"You do?" he asked. He smiled slowly. "You do?"

"I do."

They got to their feet at the same moment, their gazes locked. Tander's cane, hanging over the back of his chair, was forgotten. The hot, fragrant food on their plates was forgotten. Everything but each other was forgotten.

Tander pulled Amnity into his arms, holding her tightly to him, savoring the feel of her softly curved body nestled against him.

She loved him, he thought incredulously. Amnity Ames was in love with him. She was putting aside the pain caused by her father and brother and was trusting, believing, loving *him.* She was his . . . forever.

He claimed her lips in a searing kiss, his tongue delving into her mouth to meet hers. Hot desire rocketed through him, and his arousal was instantaneous, aching for the sweet haven of Amnity's femininity.

Oh, Tander, Amnity's heart sang. He loved her. He'd said it, and she believed him, trusted him. She was his, he was hers, and the future was a vibrant, sparkling rainbow.

"I want you, Amnity," he whispered, his lips against hers. "I want to make love with you."

"Yes. Oh, yes, Tander, I want you too. I do love you so very much."

He kissed her again, then encircled her shoulders with his arm, tucking her close to his side. They left the dining alcove and started across the living room toward the bedroom.

Suddenly, Amnity stopped, causing Tander to do the same.

She looked up at him questioningly. "You're not limping." She glanced back to where his cane hung on the chair, then met his gaze again. "Your cane is over there, and you're not limping at all."

Dear Lord, Tander thought, what was he doing? Where was his mind, his common sense? He'd been swept away by passion and the incredible revelation that Amnity loved him. He'd focused totally on the two of them, and the lovemaking they were about to share.

He'd been going to tell her the truth about

everything—his assignment for Vince, Andrew's diamond smuggling, all of it. He still intended to tell her. He had to. *Before* they made love.

He gripped her shoulders and turned her to face him. "Listen to me, Amnity. Please, just listen. I was planning on telling you every bit of this tonight, I swear it, but from the moment you said that you loved me, that's all I was concentrating on."

"Tell me what?" she asked, her voice trembling. "Why aren't you limping, Tander?"

"Because there's nothing wrong with my knee," he said, a muscle jumping along his jaw. "There never was."

"You lied about your knee, about being in an accident?"

"Yes, but—"

"You lied?"

He gave her a small shake. "Don't say it like that, with such a stricken expression on your face. Please give me a chance to explain. Amnity, years ago, I was an agent for the government. I worked in foreign countries and . . . That's not important. I retired from that life, and kept myself busy with various investments I have. Then my good friend Vince Santini quit the L.A. police force and became a private investigator. He works closely with the feds on some cases, and he asked me to take on an assignment here."

"You're working on a secret assignment for the government? You're an agent?"

"For now. It's nothing I intend to take up full time again, believe me."

"The limp was part of your cover, right? Yes, of course it was," she answered herself. "That isn't exactly a lie in the real sense of the word, is it? No, it's not. You were doing your job, an important job. You didn't lie to me. Not really. Did you, Tander? Oh, God, Tander, I don't have anywhere to put this." Tears spilled onto her cheeks.

He groaned. "Don't cry. Please, don't cry. I've loved you practically from the first minute I saw you. I was going to explain everything to you, but . . ." He pulled her close, wrapping his arms tightly around her. "Don't cry."

"I love you, and you love me," she said in a rush of words. "That's what's important . . . our love. We love each other, trust each other. Your lies . . . No! They weren't lies. They were . . ."

"Amnity, calm down. Stop it, please."

She flung her arms around his neck, gazing into his eyes. "Make love with me, Tander. Now. I only want to think about us, our love for each other. I only want *you.*"

No! his mind yelled. He had to tell her all of it. She had to know that he was there to catch her brother red-handed, that Andrew planned on using her. He had to tell her that his coming to the Crazy Quilt was calculated, their meeting preplanned and contrived. He had to clear the last of the lies from the path.

She pressed herself against him, her lower body molding to his. The tip of her tongue feathered over his lips, and she threaded her fingers through his thick hair.

"Love me, Tander," she whispered. "Don't talk anymore. It's all right, what you said about your knee being hurt, because I understand. Don't you want me, Tander? Don't you want to make love with me?" She moved erotically against his arousal with a slow, rocking rhythm of her hips. "I love you so much."

"Amnity, I . . . Oh, God."

His control snapped, and with a moan that seemed to tear at his soul, he swept her up into his arms and carried her to the bedroom.

Five

The bedroom was a rainbow.

Bright pillows dotted the white eyelet spread on the double bed. The colors were repeated in the tiebacks on the eyelet curtains, and on the whimiscal stuffed duck, mouse, and bear that were perched on the deacon's bench against one wall. The furniture was white wicker, the carpeting kelly green. The small lamp on the nightstand cast a rosy hue over the entire room.

Tander set Amnity on her feet beside the bed, then kissed her deeply. The colors of the rainbow room seemed to swirl around them in a sensual mist, creating a private world that contained just the two of them.

"You're so beautiful," Tander said as he slipped her clothes off her.

"So are you," she whispered.

He stripped off his own clothes, then pushed the throw pillows to the floor, where they lay like bright wildflowers on the green carpeting. He swept back the blankets and lifted Amnity onto the cool white sheets.

She was exquisite, he thought, his heart beating wildly. So soft and gently curved, her skin like satin. She was Amnity, and he loved her. That was all that mattered now. Nothing would be allowed to enter this place they'd made for only themselves.

Amnity gazed avidly at Tander, missing no detail of his magnificent body, savoring all that she saw. His shoulders were wide, his arms long and powerful, with taut muscles. Curly hair covered his broad chest, as blond as his skin was tanned. His sinewy legs had a smattering of blond hair, too, and his aroused manhood boldly announced his want of her.

This was Tander, the man she loved. The man she would give herself to, become one with. Nothing beyond him and what they were about to share held any importance.

She lifted her arms to him. "Tander."

He stretched out next to her, claiming her mouth in a searing kiss. With a trembling hand, he cupped one of her breasts, stroking the nipple with his thumb. Where his thumb had worked its magic, his lips followed. He drew the soft flesh into his mouth, savoring the sweet nectar.

Never, he thought, had he wanted a woman as he did Amnity. But he had never been in love before.

The emotions churning within him were as powerful as his desire. He wanted to laugh with sheer joy, and weep at the beauty of the love that filled his heart and soul. He ached and burned with the need to join his body with hers, to find the pleasure, the ecstasy, that only she could give.

His breathing rough, he moved to her other breast, laving it with his tongue, suckling, tasting. His hand skimmed down her body, over the dewy skin of her flat stomach and on to the nest of dark curls at the apex of her thighs. He cradled her femininity, his fingers seeking, finding what he sought.

Amnity purred in pleasure, her eyes closing as she savored each wondrous sensation flowing through her. She slid one hand over his chest, tangling her fingers in the moist hair, then moving to his back to feel the muscles bunch and shift beneath her palm.

She was on fire, she thought foggily, the heat within her igniting a sweet pain like nothing she had ever known. The flames seemed to twist and pulse, and she tossed her head restlessly on the pillow. She wanted. She needed. She had to have . . .

"Tander," she cried, clutching at him. "Please. I want you."

"You're ready for me," he said hoarsely. "I can feel how much you want me. Amnity, I love you so much."

"And I love you, Tander. Come to me, please."

He moved over her, his weight on his elbows as he wove his fingers through her silken hair. He kissed her, and as his tongue slid into her mouth, his manhood entered her willing body.

Amnity gasped with delight as Tander came to her, filling her with all that he was. He started a slow rhythm that she matched, keeping pace as he quickened the tempo. They were one entity, soaring above reality, reaching for the rainbow that hovered just beyond them.

Amnity clung to Tander's shoulders as he thundered within her, carrying her up, and up . . . Waves of heat gathered low within her, gaining strength, pulling him even deeper inside her. She raised her hips to meet his pounding cadence, then . . .

"Tander!"

She was flung into the swirling colors of the rainbow. Tander thrust one last time, deep, so deep, then groaned in pleasure as he found his release, joining Amnity in ecstasy.

His strength spent, he collapsed on her, inhaling her fragrance as he buried his face in her hair. She wrapped her arms tightly around his back, as though never to let him go.

They drifted in sated contentment.

Finally, with what felt like his last ounce of energy, Tander lifted himself off her, drew the blankets over them, and nestled her close to his side.

"I love you," he said quietly. "I've never experienced anything so incredibly beautiful as what we just shared. Those words aren't enough, but they're all I have. You're mine, Amnity, and I'm yours. Forever."

"Oh, Tander, I do love you very much. Our lovemaking was . . . I don't have the words to describe it, either, but we both know how wonderful it was. I never dreamed it could be like that. I never thought I could be this happy."

"The future is ours, yours and mine. Whatever we face, whatever comes, we stand together."

"Mmm," she said, and yawned.

"Sleep, my love." He kissed her on the forehead, then chuckled. "And when we wake up, we'll eat cold Chinese food."

"Perfect," she murmured, yielding to the somnolence that crept over her.

Moments later, Tander, too, closed his eyes and slept.

Tander woke with a start, not certain for a moment where he was. He blinked away the fogginess from his deep, dreamless sleep, then glanced quickly around. It was 2:21 in the morning, and the bed was empty.

He caught the pungent aroma of burning wood and saw a faint glow of light beyond the open bedroom door. Amnity was awake, and had restarted the fire in the fireplace. Why? Why wasn't she still asleep, curled up next to him?

He threw back the blankets and left the bed. Finding his slacks on the floor, he pulled them on, then went in search of Amnity. As he stepped into the living room, he stopped, his heart beating a rapid tattoo.

She was sitting in the rocking chair by the hearth, the bright multicolored afghan wrapped around her. Beneath it, he glimpsed a white cotton nightgown with wide borders of delicate lace at the hem, cuffs, and neck. The only light came from the fire, which cast a soft halo around her, leaving the remainder of the room in darkness.

Her skin looked like satin, he mused, and it felt like satin to his touch. Her hair shone like polished ebony in the firelight, and he could easily recall its silky texture and sweet aroma. Lord, she was beautiful. And he loved her. But why was she sitting there staring at the fire in the middle of the night?

"Amnity?" he said quietly.

She didn't stop her steady rocking, nor did she seem surprised to hear his voice. It was as though she'd been expecting him.

He walked into the circle of light, the width of the fireplace separating them. "Amnity?"

"Yes?" she said softly, still staring at the leaping flames.

"What are you doing out here? Couldn't you sleep?"

"I slept for a while, but then I woke up and came out here."

"Why? What's wrong?"

She slowly shifted her gaze from the fire to him. A knot tightened in his gut when he saw the tears shimmering in her eyes.

"Hey," he said. He walked over to her and knelt in front of her. Her folded hands rested in her lap, and he covered them with his, halting the motion of the rocker. "Talk to me, Amnity. You're obviously upset, but together we can handle whatever is wrong. We love each other, remember? You're not alone anymore. Tell me what you're thinking about."

Oh, dear God, Amnity thought. Tander was so magnificent with the firelight pouring over him. His skin looked like polished copper, his bare chest was beckoning to her to nestle against him.

His glorious thick hair was more blond than brown in the glow of the flames. She could feel the heat, the strength, and the gentleness in his hands, and remembered the ecstasy of those hands caressing every inch of her.

Oh, how she loved this man. She'd destroyed her protective walls and allowed him to capture her heart. She'd trusted him, and she loved him with an intensity and depth she wouldn't have dreamed she was capable of.

And it was wrong, all of it.

"Amnity?" he said again. "Come on. Talk to me. Please?"

She drew a shuddering breath and blinked back her tears. "I—I've been reliving what happened, what I did. You lied to me, Tander, and I couldn't bear it, didn't know what to do with it. So I refused to deal with it, refused to hear any more of what you were saying to me." She swallowed the sob that caught in her throat. "I blanked my mind of everything except my desire to make love with you. But now . . . now, I have to face it, all of it."

He tightened his hold on her hands. "I told you why I wasn't honest with you about my knee. I'm on an assignment, Amnity. I intended to tell you the whole thing—what I'm doing here, why I came to the Crazy Quilt, the reason for my finding a way to meet you."

"What?" she whispered, her eyes widening.

He shook his head, then released her and pushed himself to his feet. "I'm blowing this. Look, let me start at the beginning, okay?"

"You came to the Crazy Quilt for the purpose of meeting *me*? The lies about being in an accident, following your doctor's orders to do needlepoint, were all concocted so you could be near *me*? Dear heaven, why?"

"I'm going to explain it all right now."

"I've been sitting here, Tander, filled with such pain as I faced what I had done. You claim that you've loved me from the start, practically from the moment that we met, but you went on living the lies, limping around with your fancy cane, working the needlepoint rainbow. I forced you into telling me the truth about your knee."

"That's not true," he said, his voice rising slightly. "I came here tonight fully intending to tell you everything."

"Oh, really?" She huddled deeper in the afghan. "Just when were you planning on doing that? We were on our way to the bedroom when I realized you weren't using your cane. Is confessing lies what you consider romantic pillow talk, Tander?"

"Dammit, you're twisting this all around. I lost it, okay? You told me that you loved me, and all I could think about was that we loved each other, that we were going to make beautiful love together to seal our commitment. I started to explain things to you, but—"

"Yes, I know, I wouldn't listen. But, dear Lord, I thought all I was running from was the fact that you'd lied about your knee, your reason for being in Virginia. Love, Tander, is truth. I couldn't deal with the lies, so I pretended they weren't there. I practically forced myself on you, begged you to make love with me. Then, when I came out here to think, I knew I'd been wrong. Love and lies don't mix. The lies are too heavy, they shatter the love."

"Amnity . . ."

"No," she said, shaking her head. "There's nothing you can say that will change what happened. You lied to me, and probably would have continued lying if I hadn't confronted you about not using the cane. And now? My God, now you're telling me that there's more? You're saying that I'm involved in this assignment of yours? Just how far do you go in the line of duty, Tander? Was getting me to trust you, to love you and make love with you, all part of the program?"

"Dammit, Amnity, no. How in the hell can you think that?"

She got to her feet, clutching the bright afghan tightly around her, tears spilling onto her pale cheeks.

"How can I not think it?" she shouted. "Where does the deception stop and the truth start? Or is there any truth to be found here at all? Let me tell you a little story about truth and lies, Tander. About betrayal. I told you that my father traveled a lot. He was a computer-software salesman, he said, who had to go all over the country showing his products to corporation executives. Andrew and I were left with housekeepers after our mother died. We were very close. He was my friend."

"He was your hero," Tander said softly.

"Yes. I worshiped him *and* my father. I believed in their love for me, believed they truly wanted only the best for me.

"I was fourteen when Andrew graduated from high school and left me to go on the road with our father. Learning the software business, they said. Oh, God, what a joke."

"Amnity, don't. I know all of this. Don't

put yourself through the pain of talking about it."

"Both of them came home less and less frequently," she went on, as though Tander hadn't spoken. "Until, when I was seventeen, my father was arrested. For years he'd been involved in an international counterfeit-money ring, laundering money here in the U.S. I was devastated by his betrayal, his living lies. I turned to Andrew for comfort, and he told me he'd always be there for me, that the two of us were a team."

"Amnity . . ."

"But guess what?" she said harshly, dashing her tears away. "Andrew himself was arrested shortly after that, and named as a courier. My father died in prison. When Andrew got out two years ago, he came to see me. His plans for the future were vague, he said, and that was the last I saw of him. I keep hoping that, without our father here to influence him, he's gotten himself back on the right road. Oh, yes, Mr. Ellis, I know all about truth and lies."

He gripped her shoulders, resisting the urge to shake her. "So do I, Amnity. I love you. That is the truth. Those are words I've never said to another woman in my life. *I love you.* Truth, trust, works both ways. You're not trusting me enough to believe in my love for you. You won't listen to me, let me explain my assignment to you. Yes, I lied to you about my knee, about being told to relax by doing needlepoint. But my loving you is real, honest."

She twisted out of his grasp and slipped behind the rocking chair. "How do I know that? It's all jumbled together in a maze of lies. Tell me, Tander, why you sought me out. What do you want with me? What could I possibly have to do with a secret assignment for the government?"

"I'm trying to protect you, dammit. Once I knew you were innocent, all I could think about was keeping you out of harm's way."

"Once you knew I was innocent? Of what?"

"Of a scheme to smuggle stolen diamonds into the country, using your store as a cover."

"What! You thought that I—" Unable to believe what she'd heard, she stared wide-eyed at him, clutching the back of the rocking chair.

"Oh, yes, this makes sense," she went on after a moment. "I'm a smuggler of stolen diamonds. You lie about hurting your knee, and there you are in the Crazy Quilt, just as easy as you please. It didn't take much effort to get into my bed, either, did it? I mean, Lord, I literally dragged you in there. But guess what, almighty government agent? You've been wasting your time and—shall we say—energy, because I don't know anything about stolen diamonds. You got a roll in the hay out of this, Tander, but I doubt your superior will be impressed. I don't have your diamonds."

Tander gazed at her for a long moment, and when he spoke, his voice was cool, devoid of any emotion.

"You don't believe me at all, do you?" he said. "My declaring my love for you means nothing. What we shared in that bed means nothing. My telling you the truth means nothing. I know you're innocent. I know I love you with every breath in my body. I'm trying to protect you from being hurt by your brother. Andrew is using the padded crazy quilt you're expecting from Greece to smuggle in the diamonds."

"No," she whispered. "No. Andrew wouldn't . . ."

"Yes, he would," Tander said, suddenly weary. "And you know it. You're clinging to the thought of him because you've lost your faith and trust in me. Our love should be stronger than this, Amnity. *Your* love for *me* should be stronger. I realize you've been lied to in the past by your father and brother, but this is now, this is me. You're throwing me onto the pile with them without giving me a chance. That's lousy enough, Amnity, but for godsake, don't start believing that your criminal brother has suddenly become Mr. Nice Guy."

"Stop it," she cried, fresh tears brimming in her eyes. "I don't want to hear any more."

"You haven't heard one word I've said. You don't hear the truth when it's spoken. You're letting the ghosts win, destroy all we have. Our love, our future, everything, and I don't know how to keep it from happening."

He drew in a deep breath, looking up at the ceiling. "I love you," he said hoarsely. "You are the fulfillment of every wish I might have made on a million rainbows." He shifted his gaze to the fire, struggling to regain control of his emotions.

Finally, he looked at Amnity again. "I'll leave you alone for now, but I intend to follow this assignment through. I'll be watching your store, and when I see the package delivered, I'll contact you and tell you what the next step is."

He started toward the bedroom, then stopped and faced her again. "Look at that afghan you've wrapped around yourself, Amnity. It's the colors of a rainbow, but I don't think you even realize that, any more than you recognize love and truth when it's yours for the taking. We could have it all, you know. We could make wishes on rainbows together, for the rest of our lives." He shook his head, then went into the bedroom.

Amnity pressed one hand to her lips to stifle a sob. Confusion and pain coiled within her like a cold fist. Images of Tander and of Andrew danced before her eyes, intertwining, meshing. She was filled with icy misery, and the greatest fear and loneliness she'd ever known. Her world was crumbling, leaving her nothing but heartache.

She wanted Tander to be real, honest, all that she'd believed him to be. She loved him so much. Why had he lied to her? Why had he destroyed her wishes on rainbows? Oh, Tander, why?

He walked back into the room fully dressed and crossed to the front door. He stopped with his hand on the doorknob.

"I'll keep out of your way as much as I can," he said quietly, "but I do intend to see this business with the diamonds through to its proper end. I'm sorry if I've hurt you. That was never my intention. But you've hurt me, too, Amnity. I thought we had it all, the kind of love that lasts forever. If you could love me as much as I love you, trust and believe in me, we . . . Well, you can't, can you?" He opened the door. "I'll be out of your life in a few days, but you'll be my life for all time. That's just the way it is. Good night . . . my love." He left the cottage and closed the door behind him.

"Tander?" she whispered. "Oh, God, Tander, I love you so much."

She stumbled across the room to seek solace in her bed, tears blurring her vision.

The rainbow-colored afghan lay on the floor by the fire, forgotten.

Six

During the following days, Amnity felt as though she were moving in a gray mist of misery. She had a strange sense of having stepped away from herself, and was watching a smiling, efficient Amnity Ames perform her duties at the Crazy Quilt as she always had.

But Amnity, the woman, was caught in a web of confusion and heartache that caused her to wake in the night to find tears on her pillow. A cold emptiness gnawed at her, an emptiness only Tander could fill.

She loved him. She hated him. He was the source of the greatest joy she'd ever known, and the man who had shattered her heart.

To add to her growing confusion, she had to endure the echo of Tander's accusation that she had betrayed *him* by not loving him or trusting him as much as he did her.

She had hurt *him*, he had said, pain evident in his voice. She had destroyed their future, all they could have had. He would be out of her life soon; she would be his life for all time. *Good night, my love.*

Confusion. Heartache. They wrapped Amnity in a heavy shroud, leaving her exhausted.

And if that wasn't enough, there was Andrew. Where had be been in the past two years? she would wonder. Had he reformed, settled into an honest way of life? Or was he still his father's son, preparing to betray her yet again, as Tander claimed?

Confusion. Heartache.

On Monday morning, Amnity stared at her reflection in the bathroom mirror, frowning as she saw the purple smudges of fatigue beneath her eyes.

"Shape up, Amnity Ames," she told her image.

Much of the pain she was suffering, she realized, had been born of unanswered questions and crushing doubts. If she was ever to regain control of her life, she had to find those elusive answers.

She lifted her chin as she left the cottage, forcing herself to walk with firm steps. She was Amnity Ames, owner of the Crazy Quilt, she told herself. She was a woman, not a child. She would survive, face the future with dignity and class, even if that future contained no rainbows. Even if that future held only bittersweet memories of Tander Ellis.

Early Monday morning, Tander parked his car where he could easily observe, without being seen, the comings and goings at the Crazy Quilt.

Sometime after he'd left Amnity's cottage that dreadful night, he'd shut down his mind, refusing to think beyond watching for the delivery of the package from Greece.

To think was to feel. To feel was to suffer the greatest pain he'd ever known. He'd loved and lost, and whoever had said that was better than never to have loved at all should be strung up by the thumbs.

He stiffened when he saw Amnity arrive. They were separated by a hundred yards, yet in actuality, it was an expanse too great to span. What he had so briefly shared with Amnity was over.

• • •

The hours passed. Tander read the paper, studied a stock report and decided to make a few new investments, and tried not to think about Amnity.

At noon he ate the three sandwiches he'd brought from the yacht, and drank strong coffee from a Thermos.

And he waited.

Just before five o'clock, he sat up straight, every muscle tensed, senses on full alert. A brown truck with the name of a delivery service stenciled in white on the side had parked in front of the Crazy Quilt.

Adrenaline pumped through Tander's body as he watched the uniformed driver slide open the side panel on the track. The man checked his clipboard, then reached inside the truck.

"Three boxes, kid," Tander said under his breath. "One from Ireland, one from Spain, and the big bad news from Greece. Do it."

The driver of the truck did it. He straightened and headed for the front door of the Crazy Quilt, balancing his cargo, his clipboard tucked under one elbow. His arms encircled a large, square box. On top of it was a long flat box, and a small, squat one teetered on top.

Bingo, as Vince would say, Tander thought. The quilt from Greece was obviously in the big box on the bottom. The Irish linen would be in the flat one, the silk embroidery thread from Spain in the top package. This was it.

A shudder ripped through him, and his heart thudded painfully.

"Ah, hell, Ellis," he said, opening the car door, "get it in gear."

The delivery truck sped away as Tander limped toward the Crazy Quilt, leaning on his carved wooden cane.

Amnity stared at the three boxes sitting in a neat stack on the counter. She had the ridiculous notion that if she concentrated hard enough, the packages would disappear.

Tander, she knew, was outside somewhere. He was aware by now that the boxes had arrived. He was . . .

The copper bell over the door tinkled.

He was there.

Amnity felt her knees tremble. Her heart beat wildly as her mind echoed one message over and over. *I love you, Tander. I love you, Tander.*

He started toward her, and a chill swept through her. The declaration of love was pushed aside by fury.

Tander was limping. He was using that damnable cane, maintaining his disguise in front of everyone. Even her. Tander Ellis was a talking, walking, living lie.

She lifted her chin. "Tander," she said coolly. "I've been expecting you."

And he'd been missing her, aching for her, Tander thought.

"I'm here," he said, just as coolly. His gaze flickered over the boxes. "Cracker Jack time. The prizes arrived."

"Clever, Mr. Ellis." She wanted him to hold her tightly in his strong arms, to kiss her and chase away the misery within her, filling her with the warmth of his love. "I presume you have orders for me that I'm expected to follow?" She paused. "You may speak freely. There's no one else in the store at the moment."

"You're a private citizen," he said quietly. "I can only ask for your cooperation on behalf of your government. This isn't a police state. If you refuse to allow me to stake out the Crazy Quilt from the inside, I'll have to make other plans. It's entirely up to you."

"But—but you're asking me to make it possible for you to . . . What I mean is . . ." Her voice trailed off.

"Make it possible for me to apprehend your brother?" he said, his voice harsh. "You know he's coming, don't you? You're expecting him to show up here every bit as much as I am." He glanced at the packages, then met her gaze again. "And you know exactly what he's coming for. The big box on the bottom is the quilt from Greece, right? The quilt that contains the stolen diamonds. Andrew Ames is going to arrive right on schedule to get the diamonds. Right, Amnity?"

"No. No, I never said that."

"But you know it's true."

"No."

"For godsake, Amnity." He shook his head. "Forget it. You don't listen to what I have to say, anyway. Okay, bottom line. Do I have your permission to stay in the Crazy Quilt after you close for the night?"

"I'm not closing. Well, I am, but the quilting class starts tonight from seven to nine. There's a large room in the back where I hold the classes."

"Okay, I attend the quilting class. And after that?"

She looked at him for a long moment. "All right, Tander," she said slowly. "You may remain in here after the class is over."

"Fine."

"Providing that I stay with you."

He narrowed his eyes. "No way. Andrew Ames is considered armed and dangerous. There are three outstanding arrest warrants on him in California. The diamonds are the frosting on a very busy, but not very pretty, cake he's baked. He's not going to take kindly to being tripped up. I can't allow you to be in harm's way."

"You can't allow . . . Damn you, Tander Ellis." She stalked around the counter to stand directly in front of him. "If I choose to stay in my shop after nine o'clock, buster, then that's exactly what I'm going to do. As you so eloquently put it, this is not a police state. It's a free country. If I choose to camp out in my store, then, by heaven, I will. That is, in fact, precisely what I intend to do."

"Dammit, Amnity—"

"Shut up, Ellis," she said, planting her hands on her hips. "Just shut up."

Tander opened his mouth, blinked, then clamped it shut again. Oh, Lord, he thought, she was sensational. An angry Amnity Ames was an incredibly beautiful woman. Her cheeks were flushed, her eyes clear and bright. Her fury was causing her breasts to rise and fall rapidly. How sweet and lush those breasts had been in his hands, his mouth, pressed against his bare chest when they'd made love.

A smile of remembrance crept onto his lips.

"Don't you dare laugh at me, Tander Ellis," she said, snapping him out of his sensual reverie.

"I'm not," he said quickly. "I wasn't. I wouldn't."

"Now hear this . . ." she started.

"Now hear this?" he repeated, beginning to laugh. "Oh, Lord, I love it. You're really something when you get going."

"You are the most despicable, the most infuriating man I've ever met!" And she loved him so much, but she was confused, and tired, and a breath away from bursting into tears. No. She wouldn't cry. She didn't care what Tander did, or said, she would not cry. "Listen up. I'm closing the shop at six o'clock, going out for a sandwich, then returning in time to meet the students for my quilting class. You can stay, go, or take a flying leap. I really don't give diddly-squat what you do. Just don't look at me, or speak to me, or—"

He kissed her.

He dropped the cane, gripped her shoulders, hauled her to him, and brought his mouth down hard on hers.

He had not intended to kiss her, he was just suddenly doing so. She'd been telling him what to do with himself, and looking so damn beautiful he couldn't resist.

And the kiss was fire.

Passion, anger, confusion, loneliness, and love churned within them, bursting into flames of desire that threatened to consume them.

The kiss was rough, hungry, intensifying

with every passion-filled beat of their racing hearts.

The kiss was a plea from troubled minds and souls for the world to disappear and allow them just to live and love.

But the weight of the world was too great. It crushed into dust the brilliant rainbow that waited for them in the haze of passion.

The rainbow was gone, and the kiss was sadly, heartbreakingly wrong.

Tander lifted his head and released his hold on her shoulders.

"I'm sorry," he said huskily. "I shouldn't have done that. I . . . Dammit, Amnity, I love you, and I despise this whole mess we're in. It's like a bad movie."

She brushed tears from her cheeks with trembling hands. "But it's not a movie," she said, her voice unsteady. "It's very real, and very painful. I love you, Tander, but I don't like you. I hate the lies and deception, and that hate keeps pushing the love further and further away. I'm so confused, so . . ." She shook her head. "Leave me alone, Tander. Please, just leave me alone."

Many years ago, Tander had been jumped in a twisted alley in some forgotten Middle Eastern city. There had been a slipup in an assignment he'd been working on with Vince, and the wrong people had got wind of his meeting with a double agent.

It had all fallen apart. The double agent had been killed, and Tander had been badly slashed across the ribs and left for dead.

He'd lain there, in agony, he remembered, feeling his life's blood oozing from his body. Helpless, unable to move, he'd been at the mercy of events he couldn't change, or control. He'd nearly given in to the inevitable when Vince arrived like an avenging angel, and carried him to safety.

In time, the memory of the pain of that knife slicing into his flesh dimmed, but was never totally forgotten. Yet it was nothing, Tander thought, his gaze riveted to Amnity's tearstained face, compared to the pain within him at that very moment.

He was again helpless to change what was happening. He had no control over the events causing his anguish. It was as though his life's blood was once more being drained away, leaving him weak and defenseless.

This was pain of a magnitude and depth like nothing he had ever known before.

"Okay," he said, his throat tight with emotion. "I'll leave you alone, Amnity. I won't touch you or . . . I'll keep out of your way as much as possible until this thing is wrapped up." He picked up the cane. "I'm sorry."

He walked to the counter and examined each of the sealed boxes, then placed them in a row on the top of the counter.

"Leave them like this," he said, not looking at her. "Don't open them. The postmarks are clear. There's no mistaking what came from where. I'll go into the back now."

"Shall I bring you a sandwich?" Amnity asked. This was insane, she thought. She was in the middle of a living nightmare, seeing her hopes and dreams slip through her fingers like particles of sand, and she was asking Tander if he wanted a sandwich.

"I'm not hungry," he said. "You go ahead. I'll stay here."

"All right." Oh, dear Lord, she loved him. Tander . . . "Are you positive you don't want something to eat?"

"No, thank you."

She quickly closed up the shop, grabbed her coat, and fled.

Tander remained by the counter for several minutes, gripping its edge so tightly his knuckles were white. Finally, he swallowed heavily and walked into the back room.

"We have a few minutes remaining," Amnity said, "before this first class is completed. Remember that your assignment is to practice the stitches on your material swatches, and bring all that you've done with you to class next week."

Next week, her mind immediately echoed. Seven days, and nights. Where would Tander be in a week? How far away, and doing what? When she taught the class next time, she'd look at the chair where he now sat and it would be empty. He would be gone. Forever.

She cleared her throat and pulled her gaze from Tander, who was staring directly at her.

"I've shown you," she went on, smiling at the dozen women in the room, "just a few of the multitude of quilt patterns. You've seen the log-cabin pattern, Chinese puzzle, road to Oz, star of Bethlehem, a wedding quilt, and the dove in the window."

"I want to do a crazy quilt," Melissa Ferguson said. "I have a dresser drawer full of material, and each one has a special memory. I've been saving them for years with the idea of someday making them into a quilt. Will I be able to do a crazy quilt, Amnity?"

With or without stolen diamonds sewn into it? Tander thought dryly. The class had been interesting, and Amnity obviously knew her stuff. But, oh, Lord, it was agony sitting twenty feet away from the woman he loved— and couldn't have—while he kept a bland expression on his face.

When Amnity had held up the wedding quilt, he'd nearly croaked. He'd wanted to jump to his feet, tell the women to all work together to make one of those with the interlocking rings, and give it to him and Amnity as a wedding present. Fat chance.

"Yes, Mrs. Ferguson," Amnity said, "once you master the stitches, a crazy quilt will be a fine project. Crazy quilts are—she glanced at Tander, then looked back at Melissa—"*were* my favorite. They have so many hidden stories to tell." Like how one hoarded stolen diamonds? Oh, please, Andrew, no. "Well, our time is up. I'll see you all next week. Thank you for coming, and good night."

With a bustle of activity, chatter, and laughter, the women filed out of the room. Amnity followed to lock up behind them.

Tander stood slowly, then laid the cane across his chair. As he readjusted the gun nestled at the back of his belt, he heard Amnity say a final good night and close the door.

A heavy silence fell over the store.

Amnity returned to the classroom but avoided looking directly at Tander.

"Now what?" she asked.

"You go home," he said.

Her gaze collided with his. "No."

He sighed. "I didn't think so, but it was

worth one more shot. You shouldn't be here, Amnity." He held up a hand as she opened her mouth to reply. "Okay, okay, you're staying. Let's turn these lights off. Leave the night-lights on in the front, then we'll get as comfortable as possible in your office. It has the best view of the store and counter."

"Fine."

A few minutes later, they were settled in chairs in Amnity's dark office, the night-lights casting only enough glow to silhouette them in shadows.

"You're to follow my instructions to the letter," Tander said. "No arguments, just do as I tell you."

"Yes, sir," she said coolly. "Whatever you say, sir."

"Hell," he muttered.

The time ticked by with agonizing slowness. Tension was a nearly palpable entity.

Ten o'clock. Eleven. Eleven-thirty.

Amnity yawned.

"Go home," Tander said.

"No."

Twelve o'clock. One.

Amnity sighed and yawned again.

"Go—"

"No."

"Hell."

"Same to you."

At 1:42 A.M., Tander stiffened in his chair.

"What?" Amnity asked, instantly alert.

"There's someone working on the back door lock," he said quietly. "Get over here against the wall, out of the light." He stood and pulled the gun from his belt. "Not a sound, Amnity. If this is Andrew, I have to wait until he actually picks up the box from Greece."

"You don't know that it's Andrew who's—"

"Shh. Move."

Amnity did as instructed, her heart racing as she heard the back door to the store open. It clicked shut, and her knees shook as she heard the sound of footsteps coming closer.

Her mind felt as though it had shattered into several pieces, each with its own voice and fear.

Tander, please, be careful.

Andrew, don't let it be true. Don't be in my store. Don't come for the crazy quilt from Greece.

Tander, I love you. Please be careful. Be careful be . . .

Tander flattened himself against the wall, watching the main area of the store. A man crept past the office doorway, moving on to the counter. He bent his head and looked at the three boxes, then lifted his hands. . . .

Pick it up, Ames, Tander mentally urged.

Pick up the box from Greece. Pick up the—Bingo!

He strode from the office, flicking the switch on the wall and bringing the bright lights to full power. Bracing his feet, he grasped his gun in both hands, the weapon at the ready.

"Hold it right there," he said in a low, deadly voice. "Put the box back on the counter, slow and easy. Do it."

Amnity came out of the office to stand behind Tander. Her eyes widened, and a blackness seemed to descend over her.

"Oh, God, Andrew," she whispered. "It's you. Why, Andrew? Why?"

Seven

"Hey," Andrew said, smiling charmingly. "It's terrific to see you, Aimless."

Amnity closed her eyes, fighting against her tears as her brother called her by the nickname he'd tagged on her when they were children. Controlling herself, she opened her eyes and lifted her chin.

"Ames," Tander ordered, "put the box back on the counter. Now."

"Sure, no problem," Andrew said. He chuckled. "I must say, Aimless, you're hanging out with a real macho type here." He set down the box. "I was fascinated by all the fancy stickers and stamps on that box, that's all. It's no big deal."

"Hands flat on the counter," Tander said, "then assume the position. You know the routine. Spread 'em."

Andrew did as instructed, still smiling. "You're a bit overexcited, aren't you? Who in the hell are you, anyway?"

Tander moved behind Andrew, and quickly and expertly patted him down. He removed a gun that was clipped to the back of Andrew's belt beneath his sweater.

"Got a permit?" he asked.

Andrew straightened and met Tander's gaze directly. "Do you?"

He looked like Amnity, Tander thought. Andrew had the same thick dark hair, and features similar enough to make it clear he and Amnity were related. The resemblance was even more pronounced than in the photograph he'd seen of Andrew. He was a very good-looking man, but his eyes were unnerving. They were gray like Amnity's, but cold, reminding Tander of chips of icy flint.

He would like just ten minutes alone with this grinning sleazeball. Andrew Ames was one of the major obstacles on the path between him and Amnity, and he would be only too happy to remove Andrew with a less-than-gentle touch.

"Why, Andrew?" Amnity asked, her voice quavering.

"Why what, sweetie? Why did I come to see you? Hey, I missed you, kiddo. I just celebrated my birthday, you know, and I found myself taking stock of my life. You and I are family, Aimless. We only have each other, and I realized that I needed to see you, touch base with you, let you know that I love you. I'm tired of wandering around the world, Amnity. I do need you, need your kind of stability and values."

"Oh, Andrew." She shook her head. "I don't know what to think, what to believe."

"I'm trying to get myself on the straight track," Andrew said. "You're the only one I can turn to, the only person who can help me. Remember how great it was when we were kids, before I got all messed up? You and I were best friends. Remember when—"

"Knock it off, Ames," Tander interrupted harshly. "You seem to be forgetting that your brotherly visit is taking place in the middle of the night. There are outstanding warrants on you for fraud in California. A couple of nice gentlemen from the FBI will be here soon to make this all official, then I'm taking you back to California."

"This is why I showed up in the middle of the night, Amnity," Andrew said. "I was going to surprise you when you opened the store in the morning. I knew there were warrants out on me on trumped-up charges in California. I couldn't risk walking in here in broad daylight. I'll clear up this jazz on the Coast and be back before you know it. We'll start fresh, you and I, be a family like we're supposed to be."

"Right," Tander said dryly. "You're only here for a touching little reunion. You don't have any interest in that package from Greece."

Andrew frowned. "I don't know what you're talking about. I told you why I picked up that box. I don't have any idea what's in it."

"Save it." Tander took a small black metal box from his pocket and pressed the red button in the center three times. "We've got you six ways to Sunday, Ames. You're going to be held on suspicion of smuggling stolen diamonds into this country. That quilt from Greece will be thoroughly examined while I'm taking you back to California."

"Diamonds?" Andrew said. "Quilt from Greece? You're blowing smoke, man. I don't know anything about diamonds from Greece."

"Are you telling the truth, Andrew?" Amnity asked him. "You did pick up that box, you know. Please, don't lie to me, Andrew, not this time. It's too important to me."

"Amnity," Tander said, "don't do this to

yourself. He's lying through his teeth. The feds will X-ray that quilt, find the diamonds, and that will be all she wrote. Don't fall for his phony spiel about needing your help to go straight. It's all a crock."

"But—" Amnity started, only to be interrupted by a knock at the front door.

"Would you let them in, please?" Tander asked her.

"Yes, of course," she said, starting toward the door.

"Amnity, wait," Andrew called. She stopped and turned to look at him. "I'm innocent, Aimless. You'll see. I don't know anything about stolen diamonds in a quilt, I swear it. This guy is lying. I only came to see you. I'll clear up this misunderstanding in California and come right back here. We've got a lot of lost time to make up for."

"The door, Amnity," Tander said.

"Yes." She went to the door and opened it to two men wearing suits and ties. They flashed badges under her nose and strode past her.

Not bothering to close the door, Amnity pressed her fingers to her throbbing temples, watching the two men confer in low tones with Tander.

Confusion beat against her tired mind. Andrew sounded sincere. He wanted the two of them to be a family. He wanted to start fresh, to put the past behind him and begin a new life.

But the box, a little inner voice prodded. He'd picked up the package from Greece, the one with the quilt, the one with the diamonds.

And Tander was telling her not to listen to Andrew. Tander was the man she loved, but Andrew was her brother. Oh, Lord, she couldn't bear another minute of this horrible confusion.

"Nice work, Tander," one of the federal agents said. "We'll give Miss Ames a receipt for the quilt. You take Ames back to California. There's a chartered plane waiting for you at the airport. Your yacht will be on its way to the Coast with your crew whenever you give the word. We'll call Vince the minute we find the diamonds. Add it all up, and we'll put Ames away for a very long stretch."

"The hell you will," Andrew said. "Amnity, don't pay any attention to this junk. I'm innocent. The California thing is a frame, and I can prove it. And I sure as hell don't know anything about diamonds. You believe me, don't you, Aimless? Hey, this is me, your brother. These jokers are nothing to us. It's you and me, kiddo. We're family."

"Get him out of here, Hank," Tander said.

"I'll be there in a minute. I want one of you to escort Amnity home."

"You've got it, Tander," the agent named Hank said. He placed a piece of paper and a business card on the counter, then picked up the box and Andrew's gun. "There's your receipt, ma'am, along with Vincent Santini's card. If you have any questions before we contact you again, feel free to call Vince collect. We'll have your quilt back to you as quickly as possible."

"Outside, Ames," the other agent said, jerking his head at Andrew.

"Wait for me, Amnity," Andrew said, heading for the door. "I'll be back soon. I'm telling you the truth, Aimless."

"Move," the agent said.

Tander watched the three men leave the store, Hank closing the door behind them. He slipped his gun back into his belt.

"Are you all right, Amnity?"

She looked at him and gave up the struggle against her tears.

"No, I'm not all right," she said, wrapping her arms tightly around herself. "I don't know what, or who, to believe. I feel as though I'm being pulled apart. Andrew is my brother, but you're the man I . . . No, I can't think anymore. I'm so confused, and so tired."

Tander walked over to her and lifted his hand as if to stroke her face.

"No," she said, taking a step back. "Don't touch me. Don't say anything to me. I can't deal with this, can't you understand that? Go away, Tander. Leave me alone." She hung her head. "Please, just leave me alone."

Amnity! Tander yelled silently. She was falling for Andrew's phony story. They'd caught him red-handed with the package from Greece, and she was still teetering on the fence of doubt. Dammit. He had to leave her like this, take Ames back to California.

Time, Ellis, he told himself. He had to give Amnity time and space. The feds would find the diamonds in the quilt, guaranteed. She'd realize that Andrew had lied to her, as he always had. Then, Tander Ellis was coming back for his lady, his life, his love.

"I love you," he said quietly, then turned and left the Crazy Quilt.

"Oh, Tander," Amnity whispered.

Two hours later, Amnity lay in bed staring up into the darkness. She did not have any more tears left to shed. She was drained, both physically and emotionally, and felt empty, cold, and more alone than she had in her entire life.

A niggling little voice within her forced her to surface from her cocoon of depression and confusion. With a nearly detached calm, she began to replay in her mind the nightmare that had taken place at the Crazy Quilt.

She realized there had been something out of kilter, something that didn't ring true. It was lurking just beyond her mental reach, taunting her by staying hidden in the shadows. What was it?

With a sigh of temporary defeat, she finally began to drift off to sleep, telling herself she would resume her quest for the missing piece of the puzzle in the morning.

The last echo in her mind and heart before sleep claimed her was Tander's words spoken what now seemed to be a lifetime ago. *Good night, my love.*

"Tander," Vince said, "don't you have somewhere to go, something to do?"

"No."

"Go scrape the barnacles off your boat."

"No. Besides, the yacht is still in Virginia.'"

"Are you planning on spending another day here in my office, glowering at the wall?"

"Yes."

"Wonderful," Vince said dryly. "This will be day four of your charming company." He paused. "Hey, I know you're on edge because things aren't going well between you and Amnity, but waiting here for word about the quilt isn't going to help."

Tander crossed his arms over his chest and slouched lower on the sofa. "Tough. I'm not budging. I've told myself that I've lost Amnity, that it's finished. But then I think, no, dammit, there's still a chance for me. Slim, but there. Amnity was put through the wringer by me and her brother. She said herself that she felt pulled apart by what happened. I was telling her one thing, that slime Ames was dishing out the opposite."

He sat up and rested his elbows on his knees. "Vince, I know I have to pay the piper for lying to Amnity, but I can't get close enough to her at this point to start a campaign to regain her trust. Her damn brother is standing in the way. Once his guilt is proved, Amnity will have to face the fact that Andrew is still, and always will be, a criminal. Then it's between me and her. What in the hell is taking the feds so long to X-ray the quilt?"

"I don't know," Vince said.

"Call 'em."

"Come on, Tander, we've been over that fifty times. There's nothing to be gained by my bugging those guys. They have orders to report to me the minute the diamonds are found. No, I don't understand what the holdup is, but we wait, pure and simple. Go to Virginia and polish the brass on your yacht."

"No."

"Hell. You're driving me nuts, Ellis."

"Yeah, well, you weren't sunshine itself when your head was screwed on wrong about Katha. You owe me one."

"Dandy."

The telephone rang once, then stopped.

"Your secretary is quick on the draw," Tander said. He leaned back again and resumed scowling at the wall.

"Vince," a woman said over the intercom, "Hank Murphy is on line one."

"Bingo," Vince said, and snatched up the receiver. "Santini."

This was it, Tander thought, getting to his feet. This was finally it. He paced the office while Vince said nothing more than a few frustrating "I see's" that gave him no clue as to what Hank Murphy was saying.

"Dammit," Vince said finally.

"Dammit?" Tander planted his hands flat on the desk and stared at Vince. "Dammit what?"

"Would you shut up?" Vince said to Tander.

"No, not you, Hank. Ellis is giving me the crazies." He sighed, then squeezed the bridge of his nose. "Yes, we've got Ames under wraps on the fraud charges out here, but . . . dammit, I don't believe this."

"Believe what?" Tander asked.

Vince shot him a dark glare. "Hank, hold on to the quilt for one more day to give me, or Tander, time to talk to Amnity Ames. . . . Yeah, you're right, it stinks. I'll be in touch. See ya." He thudded the receiver back into place. "Dammit."

"Santini . . ."

"Tander, the quilt was clean. The diamonds weren't in the quilt. They X-rayed it, then brought in the best seamstress they could find to open, then close, the padded sections. Nothing. They found absolutely nothing."

Tander straightened, every muscle in his body taut. A wave of red fury momentarily blurred his vision.

"No, that's impossible," he said, his voice sounding strange to his own ears. "Ames is guilty. He was using Amnity and her store to smuggle in those diamonds."

"Tander, look—"

"No, you look. Ames didn't show up for a cozy reunion with his sister. He was lying to Amnity, Vince, I know he was."

"There are no diamonds," said Vince, pounding the top of his desk with his fist. "Heaven only knows where they are, but they weren't in that quilt from Greece. We've got Ames on the fraud case, but he's going to walk away from the smuggling charge scot-free. Amnity has to be told that there's no evidence to indicate that Andrew came to see her for any reason other than what he said."

Tander muttered an earthy expletive, then dragged his hands down his face.

"And I'm the bad guy," he said wearily. "Amnity's brother-the-hero is going to come across like Mr. Clean, wanting to be a family, wanting to start fresh with his sister. I'll be tagged by Amnity as nothing more than the liar who falsely accused her brother. I'll be the one she'll see as having used her for my own gain. Dammit straight to hell, Vince, Andrew Ames is guilty."

"You want him to be guilty," Vince said quietly. "The assignment is blown. We don't have the diamonds, or whoever was in on stealing them and setting up a way to smuggle them into this country."

"I want to talk to Ames . . . alone."

"No. I'm not going to let you do that. In your frame of mind, you're liable to work him over, and you'll have accomplished nothing but getting yourself into a heap of trouble."

"Vince—"

"No, you can't see him. Do you want to call Amnity and tell her there were no diamonds in the quilt, or should I do it?"

Tander walked to the window and stared unseeingly at the sweeping view of the city.

It didn't matter who told Amnity, he thought. The outcome of the newsflash that there were no diamonds in the quilt would be the same. Tander Ellis would have lost forever the woman he loved.

"Color me a coward," he said, his voice low and flat, "but I don't think I could handle hearing Amnity's voice right now, Vince. You tell her about the quilt."

"Okay. Tander, I'm sorry. I've never seen you like this. But you've never been in love before. I've been that road. It can be heaven and hell, but these things have a way of working out."

"Not this time." Tander turned and started toward the door. "Not this time, Vince."

"Where are you going?"

He stopped to look back at Vince, and shrugged. "I don't know. I guess I'll fly to Virginia, then take the yacht out and see where I end up. Take it easy." He left the office.

"See ya," Vince said quietly. "Damn."

• • •

A heavy afternoon rainstorm had caused a marked lack of customers at the Crazy Quilt, and Amnity was left to the mercy of her own thoughts.

On this, the fourth day since Andrew had made his middle-of-the-night visit to the store, she was no closer to putting a finger on just what it was that was insistently nagging at her.

Something, she thought for the umpteenth time, wasn't quite right about what had transpired that night.

With a sigh, she wandered into the large room in the back where the quilting class had been held. Her breath caught as she saw Tander's cane lying on the chair where he had left it. She walked toward it, aware that her hands were trembling as she picked up the cane.

A tool of Tander's trade, she thought. Just one of the many lies he'd told her. The hateful, damnable lies.

She ran one hand over the intricately carved wood. A tool of Tander's trade, her mind repeated. Tander had been an agent on an important assignment, and had drawn on his experience and talent to achieve his goal.

Because of her relationship to Andrew, she had been, at the onset, a viable candidate for being part of the smuggling operation. Through cunning, Tander had managed to meet her and get to know her, then had decided she was innocent. And he'd fallen in love with her.

"Oh, my God," she whispered, hugging the cane to her breasts, "what have I done?"

She'd stood in judgment of Tander. Instead of acknowledging that he'd told her the truth as quickly as he could, she'd damned him for lying to her—for doing his job.

He had been forced to pay for the sins of her father and her brother. She'd compared him to the ghosts of her past, then sent him away because she still had not come to terms with those ghosts.

She had lost the only man she'd ever loved.

Amnity closed her eyes and tightened her grip on the cane. "Oh, Tander, I'm sorry," she whispered. "It's all so clear now, and I was so terribly wrong. I love you, Tander Ellis."

But what of Andrew? her inner voice asked.

Andrew's guilt or innocence, she realized, had no bearing on her love for Tander. As her brother, Andrew held a different place in her life than Tander, the man she loved. If Andrew was innocent, she'd rejoice in his having changed his ways. If he was guilty, had betrayed her yet again, she would deal with it with a hefty measure of maturity for a change.

And what, her heart whispered, of Amnity Ames?

Tander had been right, she now knew. Her love for him should have been stronger, her faith and trust in him unconditional. She had hurt him by sending him away. Was the hurt so deep that she'd never get him back?

The sound of the tinkling copper bell brought Amnity from her reverie. She placed the cane back on the chair and hurried to the front of the store.

"Hello, Mrs. Ferguson. It's nice to see you, as always."

"Hello, dear," Melissa Ferguson said. "I'm in a dreadful rush, have a million errands to catch up on. I want an embroidery kit to give as a birthday gift. My friend loves nothing better than a new kit to work on, as she's housebound due to ill health."

A few minutes later, Melissa was bustling toward the door with her new kit.

"I hope your friend has a marvelous birthday," Amnity called.

"Oh, she will. See you soon, dear."

Marvelous birthday, Amnity thought, frowning. Birthday? Why was that striking some inner chord? Birthday.

Her eyes widened, and her heart began to pound wildly. That was it! That was the missing puzzle piece that she'd been struggling to find since that fateful night in the shop.

Andrew had said he'd just celebrated his birthday, had taken stock of his life and wanted to start fresh as a family with her. That was why he'd come to see her.

But Andrew's birthday was in August!

Eight

The next afternoon, Tander stood outside the Crazy Quilt, staring at the sign done in Old English script above the door.

During the entire flight from Los Angeles, he'd told himself over and over that he was not going to subject himself to the agony and futility of seeing Amnity. Whatever hope there might have been for him to regain her trust, rekindle her love, was destroyed.

He'd also realized during the long flight that a seed of anger was growing within him, gaining strength. He didn't know what was feeding that anger, though.

Within an hour of reaching his yacht, he had found himself in his rented car, leaving the marina. Like a cluster of iron filings being pulled by an invisible magnet, he drove in the direction of Amnity's shop.

Why? He wasn't sure. He couldn't stop himself, though, for he knew he couldn't be so close to her without seeing her one last time.

And the anger with its unknown source bubbled within him like a cauldron about to boil over.

He opened the door to the store and stepped inside. He glanced quickly around and saw no customers in the familiar, whimsical shop, then stopped in his tracks as Amnity walked out of her office.

Beautiful Amnity. In brown slacks and a fluffy yellow sweater, she looked like a ray of sunshine in the dreary, overcast day. She was his life, his love. The love he had lost.

His heart thundered and desire coiled low within him, but he didn't move. He simply stared at her, remembering all that they'd shared, thinking of what they could have had. Thinking of rainbows . . .

Amnity stopped so suddenly, she had to grab the edge of the counter to steady herself. She could barely breathe, and a rushing noise in her ears accompanied the echo of her racing heart.

Oh, Tander, she thought. He was wearing faded jeans, and the same white fisherman's sweater and blue windbreaker as when she'd first seen him. His sun-streaked hair was tousled by the wind, his skin bronzed by the sun. Magnificent Tander Ellis, whom she would always love. He was here. He'd come back to her.

"Hello, Tander," she said softly.

"Amnity," he said, nodding slightly. "Did Vince call you? Tell you that there were no diamonds in the quilt?"

"Yes, but—"

"Andrew's lawyer is making a pitch to get your brother out on bail on the fraud charges. Andrew will probably show up here again soon, despite the fact that he'll be instructed to stay in California until his trial. You two can get serious about the fresh start he's so hyped up about. It wouldn't surprise me if he beat the fraud charges and . . . Ah, hell, this is nuts. I don't know why I'm here. There's no point in it."

"Tander, I—"

"I'm sure you're pleased that Andrew apparently had nothing to do with smuggling in the diamonds. He didn't use you, lie to you, betray you. But I did, right, Amnity? That's how you see me, right? As the liar, the user. Andrew's innocent, so I'm guilty. I told myself not to come here, not to set myself up to get slam-dunked by your accusations and—"

"Tander, would you just shut up," Amnity said in a loud voice, "and let me get a word in edgewise?"

"No." He turned and started toward the door. "I don't want to hear it all. Have a great life with your beloved prodigal big brother."

"Damn you, Tander Ellis!" she yelled. "You're being infuriating again. You stop right there, mister, and let me speak."

He halted and whirled around, stunned by her outburst. He opened his mouth to retort, then realized he had no idea what to say.

Amnity took a deep breath, and her voice was quiet when she spoke again. "Tander, I love you. You're the only man I have ever, will ever, love. I'm—I'm asking you to forgive me for standing in such harsh judgment of you. You were doing your job to the best of your ability, and I should have respected that. Instead, I acted like a spoiled child who'd decided you'd broken the rules, hadn't acted the way I'd decided you should. I was wrong, Tander, and . . ." Her voice began to tremble. ". . . and I'm sorry. I love you and need you, and I can't bear the thought of losing you.

Please forgive me, Tander. *You're* the one I want to make a life with. *You're* the one I want to share the rainbows with."

"Oh, Amnity," he said, his voice raspy with emotion, "I don't believe this. Yes, I do, because you're saying it. You have a chance to have a fresh new relationship with your brother, but you're putting me, us, first." The ember of anger within him burned brighter, but he shoved it away, ignoring it. Not now, not now. "Amnity, I love you so damn much. *We're* the ones who are going to start over. We're going to— Come here."

He opened his arms to her, and she went. She ran across the room and into his embrace, burying her face in the crook of his neck as he wrapped his arms tightly around her. She lifted her head to meet his gaze.

"I love you, I love you, I love you," she said.

He claimed her mouth in a hard, searing kiss, his tongue meeting hers. He drank of her sweetness; she savored his taste, his heat, the strength of his powerful body.

"Lord, how I want you," he said. "I wish you could close the store and . . . Forget that."

"It's my store. I'll put a sign on the door saying I've closed early for just this one Saturday, and that I'll be opened again for business Monday morning."

He dropped a quick kiss on her lips. "Do it. Then let's get out of here."

It was all a blur, a wonderful, hazy, passion-laden blur. They left the store, drove their separate cars to Amnity's cottage, and once there, walked directly into the bedroom. With pounding hearts and trembling hands, they shed their clothes and tumbled onto the bed, reaching eagerly for each other.

"Oh, Tander," Amnity whispered, "I do love you so much. I thought I'd lost you, I thought—"

He captured her mouth with his as one hand skimmed over her dewy skin, blazing a heated path wherever he caressed her. He blanked his mind of everything but Amnity, of what they were sharing. He thought only of the moment, and the tomorrows that were now theirs for the taking.

His lips followed the trail of his hand, suckling one breast, then the other, as Amnity purred in sensual pleasure. Her hands, too, traveled over Tander's warm skin, tracing his ropy muscles, tangling in the tawny, curly hair on his chest, then sliding lower, and lower . . .

"Amnity . . ."

"Come to me, Tander. It's been an eternity since I've felt you inside me. Take me to the end of the rainbow."

He surged into her with one powerful thrust, filling her, bringing to her all that he was.

It was glorious. In an urgent, pounding rhythm, they were lifted up and away from this world. They soared, seeking, searching, then bursting into the wondrous place where the rainbow welcomed them in all its vibrant splendor.

"Tander!"

"Oh, yes, my love, yes."

They drifted amid the colors, floating, savoring, not wishing to leave their private world. At last they returned, and Tander kissed Amnity deeply before moving off her and drawing the blankets over their glistening, cooling bodies.

They lay close, not speaking, not wanting to break the magical spell still hovering around them. Amnity sighed in contentment. Tander kissed her on the forehead as their heads rested on the same pillow.

But then the fist of anger within Tander tightened, demanding attention. He allowed it to show itself, and reveal its source.

"Amnity," he said quietly, "I have to tell you something. There can't be any secrets between us, not anymore."

She shifted her head to meet his gaze. "What is it?"

"I'm happy, I really am, that you placed us first, before Andrew. But I have to deal with some anger, too, that our love, your love for me, wasn't strong enough to put us first before you knew whether or not there were diamonds in the quilt. I realize you want to share your life with me, even though it appears that Andrew is innocent, but . . . No, forget it. It's old news now. My anger is petty, misplaced. I won't give it room to grow. It won't be a stumbling block in our path."

"Tander, I need to tell you something too. This is so difficult for me to face. I didn't say anything to Vince about it when he called because I'm not positive it means anything, but it's nagging at me, making me doubt."

"Doubt? What do you doubt?"

"Andrew's innocence. Tander, he said he'd just celebrated his birthday, and had taken stock of his life." She paused. "Andrew didn't just celebrate his birthday. His birthday is in August."

"What?" Tander asked, frowning.

"He lied about his birthday. He was obviously ad-libbing. Because of that, my doubts keep growing. What other lies did he tell that night? Did someone slip up? Did he fully expect to have the diamonds discovered in the quilt because that was the plan? Was he blathering on to me to buy himself time to try to figure out how to make it appear he was innocent?

"Oh, Tander, I have this nagging fear that keeps saying Andrew could be guilty of everything you accused him of. I just don't know what to believe."

She could feel the tension in Tander's body and looked at him questioningly. He stared back at her, his eyes fathomless, then he left the bed and began to drag on his clothes.

She sat up, clutching the sheet over her bare breasts. "Tander, what are you doing? You're so angry I can feel your fury as though it's pouring out of you. What's wrong?"

"What's wrong?" He laughed, a sharp bark that held no humor. "I confessed that my male ego was bruised because you didn't place me and our love first right from the start. But that's okay, I told myself, I'll deal with it, because, after all, you're convinced that Andrew's innocent of using you and your store, innocent of betraying you. You chose us over him."

"But—"

"What a joke. You still have doubts about Andrew's innocence. You didn't put us first, him second, not for a minute. All this"—he swept one arm through the air—"was your ace in the hole. You're waiting for the verdict on Andrew to be absolute. You've got him in one hand, me in the other, covering all your bases."

"No! No, Tander, that's not true."

"God, what a fool I've been. You're still weighing and measuring, deciding which way to shift your emotions. Dammit, I can't live this way. What happens if no evidence ever turns up to convict Andrew on the smuggling charges? What if he beats the fraud rap and shows up here again, doing his old song and dance about needing you, wanting to be a family, telling you it's just the two of you from here on out? What then, Amnity? Do you dump me so fast I'll never know what hit me?"

"No! Tander, how can you say these things? I love you. I want to share the rest of my life with you."

"Bull. You're keeping me dangling like a marionette, deciding which way to jerk me around, waiting to see if you'll settle for me if your doubts about your brother prove right. Well, guess what, lady? I don't play second string for anyone, especially for the only woman I've ever—"

He stopped speaking and jammed his feet into his shoes, leaving his socks on the floor.

"So much for wishes on rainbows," he said, a rough edge to his voice. "I'll stick to reality from now on, that's for damn sure. I daydreamed like a stupid kid about what we could have together for a lifetime. What we . . ." He dragged one hand through his hair and took a breath so deep it seemed to tear at his soul. "Good-bye, Amnity."

"Tander, don't go." She leapt from the bed, dragging the sheet around her. "You've got this all wrong. You *are* first in my life, the most important man in the world to me. I'm not pitting you against Andrew, because I've come to understand that you each hold a place in my life. My doubts about his innocence have nothing, *nothing*, to do with my love for you."

Tander stared at her for a long moment, no warmth, no emotion at all, evident on his face or in his eyes.

Then he turned and strode from the room.

"Tander!" She stumbled after him, but the click of the front door closing jerked her to a stop.

"Tander?" she whispered. "Oh, dear God."

This wasn't happening, Amnity told herself. She and Tander had made beautiful, exquisite love, she'd fallen asleep and was having a nightmare. She'd wake up to find him smiling at her, his mesmerizing amber-flecked brown eyes glowing with love and desire. They'd make love again and again, all through the night.

A shudder swept through Amnity, and her hold on the sheet tightened. It wasn't a nightmare. It was real. Horrifying, heartbreaking, and real. It was as though she and Tander had been granted one last stolen moment, but that was all.

She was reaping what she'd sowed, was now the one on whom harsh and wrong judgment had been passed. She, too, would never again makes wishes on rainbows.

In the middle of the next afternoon, Amnity left her cottage, unable to stay within the memory-filled house for another second. She still felt numb and empty, and wondered absently if this was how she would remain as days passed into weeks, into months, into years.

More frightening than that thought was the realization that she really didn't care.

She drove to the Crazy Quilt, intent on burying herself in work. There was paperwork that needed her attention, bills to be paid, orders to place. On that quiet Sunday, alone in her haven, her precious shop, she might even find a small sense of peace, a temporary escape from cold reality.

But memories of Tander inhabited the store, following her everywhere. With a sigh of defeat, she set about her tasks, gaining no peace or pleasure in what she did.

The forgotten boxes from Ireland and Spain that she'd shoved into a corner of her office caught her eye, and she placed them on her desk. She opened the box from Ireland and ran her hand gently over the beautiful beige linen.

Then she reached for the package from Spain and cut through the strapping tape. Unable to muster any enthusiasm, she pushed back the cardboard flaps to reveal the bright colors of the silk embroidery thread within.

At midnight, four days after Tander had stormed out of Amnity's home, he sat bolt upright in bed as the small ship-to-shore radio on his nightstand beeped. He swore, then fumbled for the switch on the device, smacking on the light in the process.

"What!"

"You broke my eardrum, yo-yo."

"Vince? Lord, you're a menace. Do you know what time it is here?"

"Not really," Vince said, "since I don't know where you are."

"Oh. Well, neither do I, as a matter of fact. Wherever this is, it's midnight in the middle of a very big puddle of water. What do you want, Santini?"

"I need you here in L.A. as quickly as you can get to a port and fly in."

"Why?"

"I don't want to discuss it on the phone."

"Forget it. I'm not working for you anymore."

"It has to do with Andrew Ames."

Tander stiffened. "What about him?"

"Let me know when you're due in, and I'll meet you at my office."

"Dammit, Santini, what's going on with Ames?"

"Just get here, Ellis," Vince said, and hung up.

Tander slammed the switch to turn the radio off, then collapsed against the pillow with a groan.

"Pushy private eyes are a pain in the butt. Forget it, Santini, I'm not budging. I don't give a damn what's going on with Andrew Ames."

Three seconds passed.

"Hell."

Tander grabbed the receiver to the telephone and hit two numbers. "Pete? How close are we to land? Someplace big enough to have an airport."

When Tander arrived in Los Angeles late the next afternoon, the city was cloaked in a yellow haze of smog. It hung heavily in the air, irritating eyes and leaving an unpleasant taste in the mouths of those who dared to take a deep breath.

Tander sat in the back of a taxicab with cracked vinyl seats, and tuned out the constant chatter of the driver.

Cab drivers, he'd once deduced, were either surly types who acted put-upon because you'd interrupted their work on a crossword puzzle, or they were motor mouths, giving the impression that the passenger held captive in the rear seat was the first human contact they'd had in six months. And they all drove like lunatics.

A leather overnight bag was perched on the seat next to Tander, representing the full extent of his packing for his command-performance meeting with Vince.

Tander had called Vince's office from somewhere in Texas that morning, and ended up telling his answering machine when he was due to land in Los Angeles.

As the yellow-coated city whizzed by the taxi windows, Tander took a mental inventory of his mood. It had not improved one iota.

He was mad as hell.

He had no objections to following Vince Santini's instructions when on an official assignment, but was none too pleased with Vince's "Do, it, Ellis" attitude about making an instantaneous appearance in L.A.

And Tander was angry with himself that he'd dropped everything and done exactly as he'd been ordered—not asked, ordered—to do. Plus, he was royally ticked off that the situation centered, somehow, on Andrew Ames, a man Tander could have cheerfully spent the next fifty years hearing absolutely nothing about.

No, he mused, he was not happy, and the first order of business would be to give Vincent Santini, private investigator cum pain in the katush, a piece of his mind.

When Tander arrived at the high rise where Vince had his office, he realized that the workday was over. People were pouring out of the building, as well as all the other skyscrapers crammed together along the street, like scurrying ants. He had the strange sensation that he was impersonating a salmon trying to swim upstream as he made his way inside.

He was alone in the elevator that took him up to the eighth floor. The outer door to Vince's office was open, but the covered typewriter indicated his secretary had been among those swimming downstream and leaving the building.

He crossed the reception area and tried the door to Vince's inner office. The knob turned in his hand, and he followed the inward swing of the door.

Then he stopped. He even stopped breathing.

Standing across the room in a flowered skirt and pale pink blouse, her hair a raven curtain framing her beautiful face, was Amnity Ames.

Tander blinked, wondering if his tired mind and messed-up psyche were playing tricks on him, pushing him right over the edge to insanity.

But, no, he realized, Amnity was there, staring at him. Not smiling, not moving, not speaking, just staring at him. A quick glance around told him Vince was nowhere in attendance.

He'd been set up, he thought incredulously. And by damn, he wanted to know why.

"Hello, Amnity," he said coldly. "I take it you cooked up this cute little number with Vince."

"Yes. He agreed to help me. I assume you're angry, but please hear me out."

Damn right, he was angry, he thought. But he was also irrevocably in love with the beautiful woman standing across the room from him.

Oh, God, he couldn't handle this. The pain, the memories, were pounding against him like punishing fists. He had to get out of there.

"Well, make it quick." Kicking the door shut, he dropped his leather bag to the floor and shoved his hands into the back pockets of his jeans. "What do you want?"

Tander was so cold, Amnity thought. So cold and angry. And gorgeous. His tan was deeper, his hair lighter. His faded jeans hugged those magnificent, muscular legs with a loving touch, and his shoulders appeared a mile wide in the green polo shirt he wore. He looked tired and wonderful, crabby and beautiful, and she loved him with an intensity that was almost painful.

"Amnity?"

"What? Oh, yes." She took a steadying breath. "Tander, Andrew is guilty of smuggling the stolen diamonds into this country."

"Do tell," he said dryly. "You and Vince went to an awful lot of trouble to get me here just so you could tell me that. So, the feds tracked down the diamonds?"

"No." She paused, running her tongue over suddenly parched lips, then lifted her chin. "No. I found the diamonds, Tander, in the silk embroidery thread that was shipped from Spain."

"What?" he asked, pulling his hands free of his pockets.

"I discovered the diamonds, and—and I called Vince. I turned over the evidence that was proof of my brother's guilt."

Nine

Amnity's unbelievable words slammed against Tander's brain, hammering at his mind in rhythm with every thud of his racing heart.

He envisioned himself crossing the room, pulling Amnity into his arms and comforting her. Yet he hadn't moved, was simply staring at her in shock. He didn't know what to say, or do.

"Lord, Amnity . . ." He shook his head, unable to find words that would have any meaning, make any sense.

"Please, Tander, just let me explain, all right? This is all so difficult for me."

"Yes, of course. Please, go ahead. I'm listening, Amnity. I won't interrupt or . . . This is so damn incredible."

Amnity crossed her arms over her chest as though she were gathering her courage and holding it within her. Her voice was soft and not quite steady when she spoke.

"After you—you left, I felt so . . . no, that's not the issue here. I went to the Crazy Quilt, and I suddenly realized I'd never tended to the other imported boxes. The Irish linen was lovely, and then I opened the package from Spain. The silk embroidery thread was beautiful and appeared to be of the highest quality, which I—Oh, Lord, I'm just rambling."

"Take it easy," Tander said gently. "Tell it any way that it comes to your mind."

"Yes, well, I picked up one of the little skeins of thread, and as I ran my finger over it, I realized there was a small lump beneath the gold wrapper that was around the middle of the thread. I thought perhaps I'd gotten poor quality thread, after all, that it was tangled in a knot under the wrapping seal. I pulled off the paper and . . ." She paused and closed her eyes.

"I'm listening, Amnity. Take all the time you need."

"I pulled off the paper," she repeated, "and there, tucked in the middle of the thread, was—was a diamond. Oh, God, Tander, I felt as though I were falling into a dark pit with no way to escape. I'm not sure, but I think I yelled, 'No, no,' or maybe it was only my mind screaming, denying what I was seeing. I don't know."

He ached to go to her, but knew she had to finish this.

"I tore at the wrappers like a madwoman," she went on, "ripping them open, sobbing as the diamonds tumbled out, one after another."

He took one step toward her, then stopped, his gaze fixed to her pale face.

"They were there, Tander, the stolen diamonds, gleaming like evil eyes, mocking me with their ugly, cold existence. I knew that Andrew was guilty. He had lied to me as he'd always done. He'd used me, and my precious shop. Andrew"—a sob caught in her throat—"betrayed me once again."

Tander started toward her another time, but she raised a hand to halt him.

"No, please, stay there. Let me finish."

He nodded, emotions rushing through him like a wild river out of control.

"Somehow—this part is rather foggy—I managed to call Vince. I was crying so hard, I could hardly get the words out. He was very patient and kind, waiting for me to calm down. He put me on hold for a bit while he called the agents who were at the store that night. Then he talked to me, just kept talking, I don't really remember what he said, until the agents came to the Crazy Quilt. They brought a woman with them who took me in hand and mothered me. The next thing I knew, I was home, and the motherly FBI agent stayed with me for hours."

He owed Vince Santini, Tander thought. Vince had taken care of Amnity because he hadn't been there. Hell, no, Tander Ellis had been too busy feeling sorry for himself, off on his yacht pouting.

"I finally regained control," Amnity said, "and called Vince again. I told him that I wanted to see Andrew, to confront him myself with the truth of what he'd done."

Tander shook his head. "Amnity, why did you put yourself through that?"

"I had to. It was time for me to grow up, to face my ghosts and accept the fact that Andrew is, like my father was—a person far removed from me in values and ethics. Andrew and I have nothing in common, except for our last name. That just isn't enough."

"No, it isn't," Tander said solemnly.

She sighed. "Vince arranged for me to see Andrew, and I flew out here. When I went to the jail, Andrew lit up like a Christmas tree. He was certain I'd come to post bail for him. I told him that I'd found the diamonds and turned them over to the federal agents. He changed right before my"—Amnity's voice broke in a sob—"eyes, became vicious and mean. He called me a stupid little fool and said his going to prison was on my conscience."

Tander swore under his breath.

"It's all right, Tander. I told Andrew that my conscience was clear, my soul at peace at long last. I owed him nothing, I said, and refused to dwell on his years of lies and betrayal for one moment longer. I told him I felt only pity for him for having followed in our father's footsteps. I left then, with Andrew screaming after me that he never wanted to see me again. What he didn't know was that I'd already made up my mind that I no longer had a brother. I'm free of him, the past, and the ghosts.

"Andrew has given a full statement regarding his involvement in stealing the diamonds and smuggling them into the country. The heist was very carefully planned to make it appear that the diamonds would be in the quilt from Greece, when they'd actually been routed through Spain and put in the embroidery thread. Andrew was confident he'd be out on bail quickly, and could come back to the Crazy Quilt to get the diamonds."

She paused, still not quite able to believe her brother's alternate plan.

"If he couldn't return soon enough, a 'friend' of his was to break into the store, trash it to make it difficult to determine what was missing, and get the embroidery thread before I had a chance to sell any of it. He actually intended to destroy my shop for his own gain. Andrew's named everyone involved, because he said he wouldn't be the only one to go to prison for this. That's—that's the end of it, Tander. Andrew, my father, all those years, all those lies, have been put to rest."

"And the future?" he asked, a knot twisting tight in his gut. "What about the future, Amnity?"

"It's mine to do with as I choose. Tander, I asked Vince if he could contact you and somehow make it possible for me to see you."

"I'm here."

"Yes. As I made my decision about Andrew, I realized that with each step I took in proving his guilt, I was firmly placing another brick in the wall separating you and me."

"Amnity, look—"

"Tander, you said you'd listen to me."

"I'm sorry. Go ahead."

"I know there's no hope for us now, because Andrew is guilty as charged. There's nothing I can do or say that will ever convince you I would have acknowledged my love for you even if Andrew's supposed new leaf had been genuine. You'll believe that because I've lost my brother, I turned to you."

Tander opened his mouth to speak, then closed it again when Amnity raised a hand to silence him.

"I have one last ghost to lay to rest, Tander. I wanted to say this to you in person. Tander, before Vince told me there were no diamonds in the quilt from Greece, I knew that I loved you first and foremost, forsaking all others, even Andrew. And Vince's revelation didn't change my heart one iota.

"You were, and are, the most important person in my life. Never second choice, Tander, never that. If Andrew had been innocent, he would have had to understand that I would help him any way I could, but my focus would be on you, on our future, our—our rainbows."

"Oh, God, Amnity, let *me* talk now."

"No, there's no point to it. I know you'll never believe what I just said. Why should you? All the evidence is to the contrary. I deserve your harsh judgment of me, because it's exactly what I did to you. I judged you unfairly in matters of lies versus truth."

She placed one hand over her heart. "But now I've said the words, spoken the truth from my heart, and the ghosts are all gone. I can only hope that in time the memories of what you and I . . . No, I've said enough.

There's something for you there on Vince's desk. Good-bye, Tander."

She started across the room.

"Amnity, wait."

"On the desk, Tander," she said, tears choking her words.

He snapped his head around to look at the desk, and Amnity ran from the office.

"No! Dammit, Amnity, don't go."

He headed for the door, hesitated, then strode to the desk. A flat package wrapped in white tissue paper was lying there. A plain white square of paper was taped to the center of the tissue. It read, "You should always believe in wishes on rainbows."

He tore off the tissue, and a moan escaped him. There, in a simple oak frame, was a completed needlepoint rainbow exactly like the one he'd started.

The rainbow seemed to come alive in his hands, the colors growing more vibrant, as though urging him to remember that wishes on rainbows represented all that he and Amnity could share in a future together.

It was Amnity's parting gift to him, her last good-bye. She was hoping he would regain the ability to make whimsical wishes on rainbows. Well, he couldn't, not without her. She was the sunshine after the storm they'd been through, the only one capable of creating a rainbow in his life.

And he was not going to lose her!

Tander carefully placed the rainbow on its pillow of tissue paper, then took off for the door at a dead run.

If he didn't catch up with Amnity before she left the buliding, he'd end up following her all the way across the country to Virginia. But if that was what it took, then that was what he'd do.

Amnity Ames was his.

"Come on, Cupid," he muttered. "Help me with one more shot, buddy."

He ran out of Vince's office and down the corridor to the bank of elevators. One set of doors was starting to close, giving him a quick glimpse of a flowered skirt.

"Hold that elevator!" he yelled, thundering toward it.

The doors swished opened, and a handsome, distinquished-looking man in a three-piece suit peered out. He was tall, his perfectly groomed dark hair sprinkled generously with silver, and held a briefcase in one hand.

Amnity stood in the center of the elevator, the only other passenger. Her eyes widened as Tander zoomed into the small enclosure.

"Lobby?" Three-Piece Suit asked pleasantly.

"Fine," Tander said. "Thanks." He gripped

Amnity's shoulders. "Amnity, you can't leave like this. There are things I have to tell you, things I need to say to you."

She glanced at Three-Piece Suit, a flush of embarrassment staining her cheeks as the man turned to get a better view of them. The doors closed, and the elevator started its slow descent.

"Tander," Amnity said, "this isn't the time or place to—"

"Yes, it is," he said. "You're here and I'm here, and that's what this is all about. You and me."

"But . . ." Amnity started, looking at Three-Piece Suit again.

"Oh, don't mind me," the man said, smiling. "I'm just the driver here. C. W. Henderson, attorney-at-law."

"Nice to meet you," Tander said, his gaze riveted on Amnity. "I listened to everything you said, Amnity. It's only fair that I have my say now. I intend to, even if I have to follow you back to Virginia."

"Tander, please, there's nothing more to say. It's all been covered."

"The hell it has," he said, giving her a small shake. "I demand equal time. That's— that's the American way, that's . . ." He looked over his shoulder at C. W. Henderson. ". . . justice in its purest form."

"Check," C. W. said. He pushed the "Stop" button on the panel, and the elevator jerked to a halt.

"What are you doing?" Amnity asked, a strange little squeak in her voice. "You restart this elevator this very second."

C. W. Henderson cleared his throat, tapped the knot of his tie, and adopted a very serious expression. He could not, however, hide the glint of merriment in his blue eyes.

"Now then," he said, "I gather that Party A, hereafter to be referred to as the plaintiff, has stated her case in its entirety?"

Tander dropped his hands from Amnity's shoulders and crossed his arms over his chest. "Correct."

"So noted," C. W. said. "Therefore, Party B hereafter to be referred to as the defendant, must, under the judicial system of the United States of America, be granted equal time for his rebuttal."

"Hear, hear," Tander said.

Amnity rolled her eyes. "This is mortifying."

"No," Tander said, looking directly at her, "this is love. This is my love for you, and your love for me. The rainbow you gave me is beautiful, Amnity, but it's worthless without you. I can't make wishes on rainbows unless you're by my side, don't you see that?"

"Tan-der," she said, the flush on her cheeks deepening. "Would you shut up?"

"No. I love you, Amnity. While I was on my yacht in the middle of . . . Forget that. I never did get a clear handle on exactly where I was. Anyway, I did some heavy thinking, once I got past being mad as hell, and depressed as hell, and—"

"The defendant is blithering like an idiot," C. W. said. "The bench insists that you get to the point."

"He can blither if he wants to," Amnity said. "People in love blither all the time, because their minds are in the blender."

"So noted," C. W. said, swallowing a chuckle. "Proceed."

Tander placed his hands on Amnity's shoulders again. "Listen to me, okay? I finally focused in on trying to understand love . . . well, not love in general, because I won't live long enough to figure that out. I concentrated on *our* love. I know where I blew it, Amnity. I figured it out."

"But—"

C. W. cleared his throat, cocking an eyebrow at Amnity.

"Sorry," she said. "I won't interrupt the defendant again." She shook her head. "This is absurd."

"No," Tander said, "this is important.

Amnity, I've never been in love before, and I got off the track. When I thought about it, I realized I'd taken a very selfish approach to love, to loving you. I figured that in order to protect our love, keep it safe and strong, I should wrap it in a—a cocoon, not allow anything, or anyone, from the outside world to intrude."

"Interesting idea," C. W. said thoughtfully, "but impossible to carry out."

"Would you mind?" Amnity said. "The defendant has the floor."

"Yes, of course. Carry on."

"Where was I?" Tander asked.

"Cocooning," Amnity said. "Oh, for Pete's sake, let me out of this elevator."

"No, no, not yet," Tander said. "Look, I'm admitting that I was insecure about being in love with you. I didn't know what in the hell I was doing, and ended up doing it all wrong. Somewhere out there in the middle of wherever it was that I was, I realized that real love, our love, was bigger and stronger than I was giving it credit for."

"I—" Amnity began.

"Shh," C. W. said.

"We've been through a helluva lot together, Amnity. Our love has been pushed to the limit, but it survived. I still love you, and you still love me. Right? You do love me, don't you?"

"Yes," she whispered.

C. W. smiled.

"See? I've got this worked through. I know that I wasn't a fallback, an insurance policy. I know now that a love like ours has room for more than just the two of us. It's so strong it can encompass other things and other people. If Andrew had been sincere in his desire to start fresh, we could have helped him together, without diminishing our love one iota."

"Oh, Tander."

"And there's room," he continued, "for our children, a whole slew of them. And, Amnity? There's room for rainbows, millions of rainbows, with wishes we'll make together on every one of them."

Tears filled her eyes, but they were tears of joy this time.

"Please, Amnity, forgive me for being so dense, for taking so long to understand love. Say you'll marry me, be my wife, my life. We'll get a house in Virginia so you can keep the Crazy Quilt. We'll have the yacht for when we want to get away. I'll concentrate on my investments, and never, ever, work for Vince Santini again. Please, Amnity, say yes. Don't make me spend the rest of my days alone. I need you, and God knows how much I love you. Amnity?"

"Oh, Tander, yes!" She flung her arms around his neck and smiled up at him, love shining through the tears glistening in her eyes.

"Case dismissed!" C. W. boomed.

Amnity nearly leapt back out of Tander's arms. "Oh, good night," she said, "you scared me to death."

"Up or down?" C. W. asked, one finger hovering over the buttons on the panel.

"Up," Tander said, grinning. "We've got a very special rainbow to collect."

C. W. pressed the button, then Tander reached out and shook his hand vigorously.

"Thanks a million, C. W."

"The pleasure was all mine. You two made my day. It's very refreshing to witness a happy ending, especially in my line of work."

The doors of the elevator slid open on the floor housing Vince's office.

"What do you specialize in?" Tander asked.

"I'm a divorce lawyer—and divorced myself. Every happiness to you both. Have lots of babies, and the wishes on your million rainbows."

Tander circled Amnity's shoulders with his arm and led her from the elevator.

"Guaranteed," he said, giving C. W. a thumbs-up sign.

"Good-bye, C. W.," Amnity said, smiling at him over her shoulder.

The doors closed, and the elevator began its downward journey, taking with it C. W. Henderson, who had a very satisfied, if somewhat wistful, smile on his face.

In Vince's office, Tander pulled Amnity tightly to him and kissed her until neither of them could breathe. Waves of heated desire swept through them, and they slowly, reluctantly, ended the sensuous kiss.

"I love you," Tander said.

"And I love you, Tander. We both made mistakes. We were both wrong."

"But now we're both right. Very, very right." He suddenly tightened his hold on her again. "When I think about how close I came to losing you, I—"

"Tander, don't," she said gently. "I could say the same thing about nearly losing you, how lonely it was, empty and cold. But that's all behind us now. It's time to look to the future."

"True, very true." He paused. "Amnity, are you really all right about Andrew? I'm grateful to Vince for being there for you. I know it should have been me. But what about your brother? How are you doing?"

She sighed. "I'm dealing with it, Tander. I can't wave a magic wand and change Andrew into something he's not, will never be. It hurts, but it's a pain that will fade in time."

"If you ever want to talk about it, I'll listen." He smiled. "Wasn't that C. W. Henderson something? We'll be telling our children and grandchildren the great story about what happened in the elevator. Yep, I sure did like C. W. Say now, I just had a thought. Is your attorney and best friend, the lovely Beth Wilson, married?"

"No, she was married very young, and it was a disaster that ended in divorce. She's concentrated on her career in the years since then." She stepped back and planted her hands on her hips. "Tander Ellis," Amnity said with a laugh, "are you planning on playing matchmaker between Beth and C. W.?"

"Hey, I owe Cupid one. He came through for me when I really didn't deserve it. Think about it, Amnity. Beth and C. W. have a great deal in common, they're both very attractive people, they— "

"Live on opposite coasts."

"Minor detail," he said, waving one hand breezily in the air.

She slid her arms around his waist and smiled up at him. "I love you, you crazy man. You were, I presume, a swinging playboy, dashing here and there with the jet set, moving in the fast lane, jaunting off to who knows where on your yacht. Now? You're about to get married, you're talking about a mortgage, babies, and to top it off, you're applying for the job of Cupid's partner."

"You betcha, kid. Once you get through the rough stuff of this love number, it's a class act, the best show in town. I, Tander Ellis, love being in love . . . with you."

"And I'm glad."

"How do you feel about getting out of here, going someplace for a romantic dinner, then . . ."

"Then?"

"I'll allow you to ravish my body."

"Sold."

"Hey, whoa. I've got to get my rainbow." He crossed the room and picked up the needlepoint, wrapping it back up in the tissue paper. "This is really nice. Maybe I'll finish the one I started, and we'll hang them as a matched set on a wall in our new house. In the meantime, let's go to—Oh, great, I just remembered that the yacht is out in the ocean somewhere with the crew, chugging in this direction. Tsk, tsk, I suppose I'll have to check into a hotel for tonight."

"Not a chance, Ellis. I have a beautiful hotel room that's been terribly lonely without you."

"A situation I'll be only too pleased to rectify, my love."

"Perfect. You know, Tander, we *will* have a million rainbows in our future, but I really don't think I'll be making any wishes on them."

He looked down at her questioningly. "Why not?"

She placed one hand on his cheek and smiled up at him, love glowing in the clear gray depths of her eyes.

"Because I've been granted the most precious wish of all. I have the love of Tander Ellis."

THE EDITOR'S CORNER

Those sultry June breezes will soon start to whisper through the trees, bringing with them the wonderful scents of summer. Imagine the unmistakable aroma of fresh-cut grass and the feeling of walking barefoot across a lush green lawn. Then look on your bookstore shelves for our striking jade-green LOVESWEPTs! The beautiful covers next month will put you right in the mood to welcome the summer season—and our authors will put you in the mood for romance.

Peggy Webb weaves her sensual magic once more in **UNTIL MORNING COMES,** LOVESWEPT #402. In this emotional story, Peggy captures the stark beauty of the Arizona desert and the fragile beauty of the love two very different people find together. In San Francisco he's known as Dr. Colter Gray, but in the land of his Apache ancestors, he's Gray Wolf. Reconciling the two aspects of his identity becomes a torment to Colter, but when he meets Jo Beth McGill, his life heads in a new direction. Jo Beth has brought her elderly parents along on her assignment to photograph the desert cacti. Concerned about her father's increasing senility, Jo Beth has vowed never to abandon her parents to the perils of old age. But when she meets Colter, she worries that she'll have to choose between them. When Colter appears on his stallion in the moonlight, ready to woo her with ancient Apache love rituals, Jo Beth trembles with excitement and gives herself up to the mysterious man in whose arms she finds her own security. This tender story deals with love on many levels and will leave you with a warm feeling in your heart.

In LOVESWEPT #403 by Linda Cajio, all it takes is **JUST ONE LOOK** for Remy St. Jacques to fall for the beguiling seductress Susan Kitteridge. Ordered to shadow the woman he believes to be a traitor, Remy comes to realize the lady who drives him to sweet obsession could not be what she seemed. Afraid of exposing those she loves to danger, Susan is caught up in the life of lies she'd live for so long. But she yearns to confess all to Remy the moment the bayou outlaw captures her lips with his. In her smooth, sophisticated style, Linda creates a winning love story you won't be able to put down. As an added treat, Linda brings back the lovable character of Lettice as her third and last granddaughter finds true happiness and love. Hint! Hint! This won't be the last you'll hear of Lettice, though. Stay tuned!

(continued)

With her debut book, **PERFECT MORNING,** published in April 1989, Marcia Evanick made quite a splash in the romance world. Next month Marcia returns to the LOVESWEPT lineup with **INDESCRIBABLY DELICIOUS,** LOVESWEPT #404. Marcia has a unique talent for blending the sensuality of a love story with the humorous trials and tribulations of single parenthood. When Dillon McKenzie follows a tantalizing scent to his neighbor's kitchen, he finds delicious temptation living next door! Elizabeth Lancaster is delighted that Dillon and his two sons have moved in; now her boy Aaron will have playmates. What she doesn't count on is becoming Dillon's playmate! He brings out all her hidden desires and makes her see there's so much more to life than just her son and the business she's built creating scrumptious cakes and candies. You'll be enthralled by these two genuine characters who must find a way to join their families as well as their dreams.

As promised, Tami Hoag returns with her second pot of pure gold in *The Rainbow Chasers* series, **KEEPING COMPANY,** LOVESWEPT #405. Alaina Montgomery just knew something would go wrong on her way to her friend Jayne's costume party dressed as a sexy comic-book princess. When her car konks out on a deserted stretch of road, she's more embarrassed by her costume than frightened of danger—until Dylan Harrison stops to help her. At first she believes he's an escaped lunatic, then he captivates her with his charm and incredible sex appeal—and Alaina actually learns to like him—even after he gets them arrested. A cool-headed realist, Alaina is unaccustomed to Dylan's carefree attitude toward life. So she surprises even herself when she accepts his silly proposal to "keep company" to curtail their matchmaking friends from interfering in their lives. Even more surprising is the way Dylan makes her feel, as if her mouth were made for long, slow kisses. Tami's flare for humor shines in this story of a reckless dreamer who teaches a lady lawyer to believe in magic.

In Judy Gill's **DESPERADO,** LOVESWEPT #406, hero Bruce Hagendorn carries the well-earned nickname of Stud. But there's much more to the former hockey star than his name implies—and he intends to convince his lovely neighbor, Mary Delaney, of that fact. After Mary saves him from a severe allergy attack that she had unintentionally caused, Bruce vows to coax his personal Florence Nightingale out to play. An intensely driven woman, Mary has set certain goals

(continued)

for herself that she's focused all her attention on attaining—doing so allows her to shut out the hurts from her past. But Bruce/Stud won't take no for an answer, and Mary finds herself caught under the spell of the most virile man she's ever met. She can't help wishing, though, that he'd tell her where he goes at night, what kind of business it is that he's so dedicated to. But Bruce knows once he tells Mary, he could lose her forever. This powerful story is sure to have an impact on the lives of many readers, as Judy deals with the ecstasy and the heartache true love can bring.

We're delighted as always to bring you another memorable romance from one of the ladies who's helped make LOVESWEPT so successful. Fayrene Preston's *SwanSea Place:* **DECEIT**, LOVESWEPT #407, is the *pièce de résistance* to a fabulous month of romantic reading awaiting you. Once again Fayrene transports you to Maine and the great estate of SwanSea Place, where Richard Zagen has come in search of Liana Marchall, the only woman he's ever loved. Richard has been haunted, tormented by memories of the legendary model he knows better as the heartless siren who'd left him to build her career in the arms of another. Liana knows only too well the desperate desire Richard is capable of making her feel. She's run once from the man who could give her astonishing pleasure and inflict shattering pain, but time has only deepened her hunger for him. Fayrene's characters create more elemental force than the waves crashing against the rocky coast. Let them sweep you up in their inferno of passion!

As always we invite you to write to us with your thoughts and comments. We hope your summer is off to a fabulous start! Sincerely,

Susann Brailey

Susann Brailey
Editor
LOVESWEPT
Bantam Books
666 Fifth Avenue
New York, NY 10103

FAN OF THE MONTH

Ricki L. Ebbs

I guess I started reading the LOVESWEPT series as soon as it hit the market. I had been looking for a different kind of romance novel, one that had humor, adventure, a little danger, some offbeat characters, and, of course, true love and a happy ending. When I read my first LOVESWEPT, I stopped looking.

Fayrene Preston, Kay Hooper, Iris Johansen, Joan Elliott Pickart, Sandra Brown, and Deborah Smith are some of my favorite authors. I love Kay Hooper's wonderful sense of humor. For pure sensuality, Sandra Brown's books are unsurpassed. Though their writing styles are different, Iris Johansen, Joan Elliott Pickart, and Fayrene Preston write humorous, touching, and wonderfully sentimental stories. Deborah Smith's books have a unique blend of adventure and romance, and she keeps bringing back those characters I always wonder about at the end of the story. (I'm nosy about my friends' lives too.)

I'm single, with a terrific but demanding job as an administrative assistant. When I get the chance, I always pick up a mystery or romance novel. I have taken some kidding from my family and friends for my favorite reading. My brother says I should have been Sherlock Holmes or Scarlett O'Hara. I don't care what they say. I may be one of the last romantics, but I think the world looks a little better with a slightly romantic tint, and LOVESWEPTs certainly help to keep it rosy.

THE DELANEY DYNASTY

THE SHAMROCK TRINITY

☐   21975   RAFE, THE MAVERICK
                by Kay Hooper $2.95

☐   21976   YORK, THE RENEGADE
                by Iris Johansen $2.95

☐   21977   BURKE, THE KINGPIN
                by Fayrene Preston $2.95

THE DELANEYS OF KILLAROO

☐   21872   ADELAIDE, THE ENCHANTRESS
                by Kay Hooper $2.75

☐   21873   MATILDA, THE ADVENTURESS
                by Iris Johansen $2.75

☐   21874   SYDNEY, THE TEMPTRESS
                by Fayrene Preston $2.75

THE DELANEYS: *The Untamed Years*

☐   21899   GOLDEN FLAMES *by Kay Hooper* $3.50
☐   21898   WILD SILVER *by Iris Johansen* $3.50
☐   21897   COPPER FIRE *by Fayrene Preston* $3.50

THE DELANEYS II

☐   21978   SATIN ICE *by Iris Johansen* $3.50
☐   21979   SILKEN THUNDER *by Fayrene Preston* $3.50
☐   21980   VELVET LIGHTNING *by Kay Hooper* $3.50

THE LATEST IN BOOKS
AND AUDIO CASSETTES

Paperbacks

☐	27032	**FIRST BORN** Doris Mortman	$4.95
☐	27283	**BRAZEN VIRTUE** Nora Roberts	$3.95
☐	25891	**THE TWO MRS. GRENVILLES** Dominick Dunne	$4.95
☐	27891	**PEOPLE LIKE US** Dominick Dunne	$4.95
☐	27260	**WILD SWAN** Celeste De Blasis	$4.95
☐	25692	**SWAN'S CHANCE** Celeste De Blasis	$4.50
☐	26543	**ACT OF WILL** Barbara Taylor Bradford	$5.95
☐	27790	**A WOMAN OF SUBSTANCE** Barbara Taylor Bradford	$5.95

Audio

☐ **THE SHELL SEEKERS** by Rosamunde Pilcher
Performance by Lynn Redgrave
180 Mins. Double Cassette   48183-9 $14.95

☐ **COLD SASSY TREE** by Olive Ann Burns
Performance by Richard Thomas
180 Mins. Double Cassette   45166-9 $14.95

☐ **PEOPLE LIKE US** by Dominick Dunne
Performance by Len Cariou
180 Mins. Double Cassette   45164-2 $14.95

☐ **CAT'S EYE** by Margaret Atwood
Performance by Kate Nelligan
180 Mins. Double Cassette   45203-7 $14.95

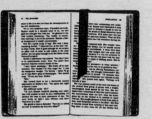